Nazi

Jazz

Porn

Brad D. Sibbersen

10 9 8 7 6 5 4 3 2

Brought to Rune
5

Everything You Ever Wanted For a Dollar
35

Dog Days
47

The Carved One
63

(Un)Screwed
71

The First Ghetto Hen Born, Booming, as an Institution
75

Emma-Sue Is a Cheap Fuck
77

Limbs
81

Hallucitopia
83

We Are the Real Children of the Corn
101

The Book of Bob
105

Sing Those Beautiful Junkyard Dues
109

Dream Surplus (The Great Molasses Flood)
117

The Song of Gretchen
119

This One's For the Dandelions, the Clover, the Watercress
127

The Stroll
133

The Phone
137

Dog In the Morning Meeting
143

Ghost of a Scene
145

Oblique
155

Their Own Little Corner of Heaven
169

Uncle Amjad's Email
173

Phonomania
179

The Little White Duck
189

Parking Lot World
195

Christmas Memories
205

Brought to Rune

The whole dreadful business began when Fanny told Sandy that he should stop calling himself a "writer" because he would never write that book, ever, and perhaps he should find some other way to impress undergraduates because his current approach clearly wasn't working. This, naturally, set Sandy off, and he was currently stalking back and forth our tiny dorm room, waving his arms about like a madman, and ranting and raving along the general lines of "Who does she think she is?" and "I'll show her!" and such. I suggested, rather rationally, I thought, that perhaps the best way to prove Fanny wrong would be to simply sit down and write the book in question. This made little impression, however. Instead, Sandy declared that the only possible solution to his current woes, the only rational solution, really, would be to get extremely intoxicated. And as his room-mate, he further insisted, I was duty-bound to join him.

This, unfortunately, presented some practical difficulties, the first being that our campus was "dry", as they say. Of course some alcohol inevitably found its way into the dorms, but as it was technically against the rules it was rarely flaunted and generally hoarded. Generosity with one's personal cache was uncommon, at best. Furthermore, undergraduates were not permitted to own automobiles, which meant that, in order to reach the nearest tavern where alcohol was served, one was forced to take the motor-bus, and, this being a Saturday, the last motor-bus between campus and town had run at four o'clock, well over an hour past. Sandy was not to be deterred however, and, after much cajoling and bargaining and application of spurious logic, he convinced me to accompany him, on foot, to the highway which bordered our campus to the north, where we would hitch our way the fifteen or so miles into town. Sighing, I donned my coat and followed him out the door.

Dusk was staining the horizon by the time a motorist finally took pity upon us and stopped, and by that time we had already walked a third of the way. The driver, a heavyset, middle-aged woman with unnaturally orange-coloured hair, kindly dropped us off right at the front door of one of the more popular local drinking establishments, where we immediately planted ourselves at the bar proper and ordered our first round of drinks, on Sandy, of course, as this entire undertaking was at his insistence and I, quite frankly, should have been studying for an upcoming classical literature midterm that I was sure to perform poorly on after losing a night to debauchery, and likely much of the following day deep in the throes of an alcohol hangover. Nevertheless, one must support one's friends, so I steadfastly ploughed ahead as Sandy ordered round after round of drinks, nodded at all the right moments as he railed against Fanny and her limited world-view, agreed vehemently when he declared that his novel, once completed, would change literature forever and show that Fanny once and for all, and, much later, nodded sagely as, behind the tavern, he expelled most of the liquor he had imbibed into the shrubbery while tearfully confessing his love for Fanny "...but you mustn't tell her, ever, Blake! You mustn't!" I agreed that I would not.

So it was that we found ourselves stumble-bumming down Main Street in the wee hours of the morning, hopelessly intoxicated, pretending that our hopes of finding a ride back to campus weren't entirely in vain. I don't know how long we continued in this manner, holding each other up – Sandy occasionally losing consciousness completely and falling to the ground, pulling me with him – but it seemed like hours, and as my head finally began to clear enough for me to take any rational stock of our situation I realized that we were now far off the beaten path, quite literally. For if the correct path was the black ribbon of highway we had original been following, we had apparently deviated from it some time ago. The track we were on now was gravel, lit only by a first-night full moon, and I was astounded that we could have come so far from the lights of the town without realizing it. "Sandy!" I whispered, "I fear we're lost!"

"Thleef," Sandy responded, waving his hand in what he apparently believed to be my general direction. Somehow, though, I understood what he meant: sleep.

"You fool," I hissed. "We can't sleep here! We'll be run over by an automobile, or die of exposure!" The latter, of course, was highly unlikely, as there was but the faintest chill in the air. But one must sometimes be dramatic with drunks; often this is all they will respond to. "We must attempt to backtrack," I continued, as Sandy slowly sank to his knees and knelt there, in the middle of the road, as if trying to decide whether to continue listening to what I had to say, or simply lie down and go to sleep. "We can't have come too far from the highway," I continued. "If we keep our wits about us I'm sure we'll find ourselves home in no time." In response, Sandy shook his head in a bizarre, diagonal manner that could have indicated yes, or no, or possibly both, and then, muttering something that might have been "Fanny", he passed out face-first in the gravel.

If you've ever been obliged to carry a drunk – literally, I mean – you know what I was faced with. A co-ed in such a state can easily be lifted into one's arms or hefted over a shoulder and, assuming one is a gentleman, delivered safety home to "sleep it off", as it were. But to carry a full-grown lad, fully in his cups, that is another thing entirely. Dead weight Sandy was, and after multiple attempts ended with me falling to the ground and him falling atop me, I finally admitted defeat and simply dragged him to the side of the road. Having exhausted my last reserve of strength I sat down heavily on the ground beside him. "Oh, Sandford," I sighed aloud. "Why must you always get us into these predicaments?" Still, I had to admit that if one were forced to spend a night outdoors when one had, in fact, a perfectly good bed to sleep in – and not so far off, really – this was certainly an amicable night on which to do so. The sky was clear and nighttime-bright, the temperature cool enough to discourage insects but not so cool as to be particularly uncomfortable, and the fresh, pine-scent of the dominating foliage, though it hung heavily over everything, was a welcome change from the dorms, with their persistent odour of sweat-smell, cigarette smoke, and pungent cleaning chemicals. Students, in the collective, produce an aromatic froth best left to the imagination, I assure you. I inhaled deeply, savouring the moment, exhaled, closed my eyes to inhale again, felt dizzy, and suddenly found myself prone, staring up at the full moon. It was just as well, I decided. Sandy's current woes would undoubtedly be obfuscated by the painful hangover he would experience tomorrow, the whole silly business with the formless novel would be temporarily forgotten, and all the chaps back at the dorms would have a good laugh over it. As for me, well, tonight's distractions notwithstanding I'd been quite prudent about keeping up with my studies, I had many good friends – like Sandy – with whom I could "cut loose" from time to time, and of course I had been seeing Fanny, on the sly, for the past several weeks, and we'd been having quite the jolly time, actually. Yes, I thought, life was good.

It seemed as though I'd been lost in thought for quite some time when I noticed a faint glow just a bit further down the gravel road, clearly that of electrical lights. Nudging Sandy I was surprised to find him somewhat responsive, so I shook him roughly until he sat up, his eyes wild and bleary, his manner confused. "Wherwe?" he slurred, one word, and I simply pointed in the direction of the light as I pulled him to his feet.

"Civilization," I explained, and he seemed to accept this, following behind me in great, galumphing steps that were likely scattering terrified wildlife for miles in every direction. We walked what must have been a quarter of a mile before the path curved and suddenly there it was, looming over us. We'd practically been on top of it the entire time we'd been sleeping by the side of a road: an inn, well-lit and and clearly open for business even at this late hour. I did not know whether to laugh or cry, so I did neither, taking Sandy by the sleeve to keep him on a straight course as we stumbled up the walk. Oh, the lads would have a field day with this one! Standing up straight, I took a deep breath, brushed imaginary dust off the front of my suit-coat, and stepped inside.

The foyer was small but charming, and smelled heavily of oak, so heavily that I suspected that what I was actually smelling was some chemical aping the scent, rather than the thing itself. Still, everything did appear to be made of wood, heavily lacquered. The room was dim, lit only by the embers of a dying fire, yet the overall impression was that of safety, warmth, and, incongruously, family. A suddenly pang of nostalgia sank its incisors deep into my heart, and I nearly wept for thoughts of Christmases past, loves lost, cosy evenings spent in rooms not unlike this one, although, oddly, no specific room readily came to mind. Behind the check-in desk an elderly man, short, heavy-set, and bald, with a thick white moustache, eyed us warily. I realized that I was swaying slightly.

"Lost are ye?" the man finally said, in an accent that sounded exaggerated, or false, and that, when I tried to place it, made me feel as if I were trying to grasp the wind.

"No," I managed, wondering why I'd lied, and I suddenly realized that I was far more intoxicated than

I had thought. Sandy, behind me, slowly and quietly crumpled to the floor and was immediately snoring on the carpet.

"You'll be needing a room then," the old man said, already writing in the sign-in book. "You can have number 13..." His demeanour darkened then, and he fixed us with a long, humourless stare that began to concern me until, his little joke concluded, he favoured us with a sly smile and, finally, laughter. "No, no," he laughed. "You look to have had enough bad luck tonight. We'll put you in number 12!"

Never has the sun been more unwelcome than when it found my eyes through the window of room number 12. It was just dawn, far too early to rise, really, even for those far more civilized and responsible than we. But drunken sleep, as those who have experienced it well know, is no real sleep at all, and I knew I would not be finding my way back to its comfortable oblivion. Better to rise now and face the day, and the consequences of our debauchery, like a man. I only hoped that the front desk would be manned at this odd hour, so that we could settle our bill and be on our way. "Why didn't you close the curtains last night?" moaned Sandy from the floor. Sitting up, I took one look at him and hoped that I didn't appear as dishevelled as he, although it was a surety that I did. His tie was askew, one cuff link was missing, his suit was coated with leaves, dirt, and loose bits of gravel, and he even had twigs sticking out of his hair. My face must have betrayed my thoughts for he snorted, smiled, and said "You don't look any better, chap."

"Well met," I replied, toasting an invisible shot in Sandy's direction. Sandy buried his face in his hands and groaned.

"Well met, indeed," he said.

"I say, what's this then?" I heard Sandy exclaim as I splashed cold water from the washbasin in my face. Stepping out of the tiny lavatory, I saw him standing in the hallway, staring at the front of the door to our room.

"What is it?" I asked, joining him.

"You tell me," he shrugged, indicating the red figures scrawled across the door at approximately waist level. Two intersecting squares, an isosceles triangle standing on one point, and two other, more complicated symbols I didn't immediately recognize. They glistened, wet, in the early morning light. "Is that... is it blood?" Sandy suddenly asked, gingerly running his index figure through the squares, leaving a red smear in its wake. Carefully, he tasted the substance. "Ugh! Paint!" I laughed at his foolishness, then caught myself.

"Look!" I exclaimed. Following my gaze he looked down the hallway. There were two other rooms opposite us, and one a bit down the hall, towards the foyer, on our side. The door to each had symbols, though not always the same ones, painted on them as well.

"What does it mean?" Sandy whispered.

"A prank, perhaps?" I ventured. "Mayhap some of our school chums have tracked us down."

"But what does it *mean?*" Sandy repeated. I dismissed him with a wave.

"Nothing. Absurdity. If it was our fellows, I suggest we check out immediately, before we're held responsible for the damage."

"Nonsense," exclaimed Sandy. "I'm getting to the bottom of this right now!" Straightening his tie, he stalked off towards the foyer, and I had no choice but to follow. We found the same old man, or his twin, behind the front desk, fiddling with a fountain pen, and Sandy strode purposefully up to the fellow, leaned heavily against the counter, arms spread wide, and confronted him. "I say, man, what's with the gibberish smeared all over our door? Is this some sort of racket? A scam to charge us for damages?" The old man opened his mouth to respond, but Sandy hardly gave him the chance. "I'll have you know, you rascal," he continued, "that my uncle is a barrister, and if you think for one moment that you can perpetrate this sort of foolishness..."

Sandy's monologue went on for some time, but just as I was considering pulling up a chair so as to sit the rest of it out he seemed to run out of steam, finally narrowing his eyes in a self-consciously dramatic fashion and glaring at the old man – who'd spoken nary a word during the entire tirade – as if daring him to respond. And respond he did, and would that I could have bottled the look of shock on Sandy's face when the old man calmly replied:

"It'll be five for the room then."

"What?!" cried my friend. "Is that all there is then?!"

"Was your stay in some way unsatisfactory?"

Sandy was shaking with fury now, and I feared he might actually strike the old fellow, though I'd rarely known him to resort to physical violence before, at least not without the aid of copious amounts of spirits. Instead, he spun and snarled sideways in my direction as he stormed past.

"Pay the landlord, Blake! I must collect my belongings!" Knowing full well that any "belongings" we currently possessed were on our person, I quickly followed him. What was he up to?

"You're not going to get up to some mischief, are you?" I hissed as we walked briskly back to the room "Vandalize the room or some such?"

"Perish the thought," Sandy replied, stopping short just outside our room. He patted down his coat and trousers, and, apparently not finding what he was looking for, cursed angrily through clenched teeth. He appealed to me, "I'll need the landlord's fountain pen. Run and fetch it for me."

"Are you daft? After the verbal lashing you gave him? He'll likely call the constable as it is! Scrawling some epithet on the walls won't solve anything. Dare I say it, you're over-reacting, Sandford, and I demand that we leave immediately!"

"Bah!" Sandy dismissed me. "Do as you will. Whatever his game is, I'll not be played for a fool!"

Just then, a strange, squeaking noise caught my attention.

"Did you hear that?" demanded Sandy. I nodded. As one, we turned in the direction of the sound, further down the hallway, only to spy the chambermaid, pushing before her a large cart full of towels, supplies for the water closet, and so forth. With each full rotation, the front left wheel of her massive cart let out a painful cry. "You there!" cried Sandy, startling the woman out of her early morning reverie. "Come here immediately!" The woman did as she was bade and, with a flourish I found a rather dramatic given the circumstances, Sandy indicated the marks upon our door and glared at her with the angriest expression he could muster.

"Well?" he demanded. "What is the meaning of this?"

"Why," the poor woman stammered (I must confess, I was quite embarrassed by the point, and hung back, suddenly taking a particular interest in the pattern on the wallpaper) "there's no meaning at all sir! Guests usually aren't up at this hour, is all. I... I'll get that wiped off in a jiffy, I will!"

"The blazes you will!" shouted Sandy. Brushing the flustered woman aside, he strode quickly to her cart and began rifling through it, scattering toiletries across the floor. Finally, he located what he was looking for: a scrap of paper (this had some simple instructions for the maid hastily scribbled on one side) and a small, stubby pencil, the type that might be given gratis to a guest should the need for a writing utensil suddenly arise. Paper and pencil in hand, Sandy studied the odd runes on our door carefully, and duplicated them exactly on his pilfered sheet.

"I say, I don't believe that is allowed, sir! Return that at once or I'll be forced to call the landlord!"

"Call your cursed landlord then!" snarled Sandy. "I daresay the old sod can just try to wrest this from me, if he thinks he's able!" Sandy shook the paper with the runes drawn on it in her face, for emphasis.

"Why, you're no gentleman!" the woman huffed, and scampered off down the hallway in the direction of the foyer.

"I hope you're satisfied!" I said. "I remind you that we're still somewhat in the grip of the drink, and there'll be no end of trouble if you don't drop this matter now! I myself don't fancy being arrested for drunkenness at..." I made a show of producing and checking my pocket watch. The crystal, I noticed with some dismay, was now cracked. "...five o'clock in the morning!"

"Balderdash!" Sandy dismissed my concerns with a wave. "This is some plot, I'm convinced of it! Well we'll get to the bottom of it now, I assure you!"

Moments later the landlord came storming into the hallway, the chambermaid trailing timidly behind. He was a much larger man than he'd initially appeared, seated behind his desk in the foyer, and at that moment I found myself more than a little intimidated. Sandy, however, stood his ground.

"The constable is on his way!" the landlord growled. "I suggest you rapscallions settle up and be on your way, or, I promise you, there will be trouble!"

"'Rapscallions'? How dare you, sir!" cried Sandy. Dramatically producing a single note from his breast pocket (where he'd stashed it only moments before, so as to be able to make this melodramatic gesture) he threw it to the ground at the landlord's feet. "Our debt is settled!" he declared. Then, holding up the sheet of paper he had transcribed the strange runes onto, be continued: "Now we will discuss *this* piece of business."

Only then did I surmise that perhaps Sandy was onto something, after all. For the landlord, shocked, turned with angry eyes towards the chambermaid, who hung her head in shame. "I'm sorry, sir," she stammered, "But I was runnin' late this mornin' and

the gent'men rose so much earlier than is usual..."
The landlord dismissed her fumbling excuses with a
wave and a "Fah!", turning back to us.

"Now that scrapt" [this is how he pronounced it –
scrapt] "of paper there is property of this
establishment, and you'll be returning it forthwith!"

"This?!" laughed Sandy. "Why, it's garbage!"

"Garbage?" said the landlord. "Why, there's
important instructions for our employees on that
sheet, pertaining as to the proper care of the rooms
insomuch and so forth. It's a legal document!"

"A legal document!" cried Sandy, at which point he
began reading the instructions in question aloud,
injecting commentary of his own as he went: "*Furst*
[This common word is spelled incorrectly.] *cleen*
[Also spelled incorrectly.] *all the bedsheets in rooms
nine and ten ... Second, scrub the floor's in all the
room's* [Not one but *two* gratuitous apostrophes here.
Perhaps this establishment purchases them in
bulk!]..." He was clearly enjoying this, and as I well
know, when Sandy is having this much fun nothing
but trouble can result.

"You making light of me, then," the landlord
growled, "because I ain't a educated man like
yourself? So educated he drinks 'til all hours and is
disrespectful to his elders and to women?" Here, he
indicated the chambermaid, who looked more
embarrassed than ever. "I'm of a mind to strike you
down boy, right here and now!" A look came over
Sandy's face then, a look that I had seen only once or
twice before. I knew then, without a doubt, that this
could only end in the arrest of everyone involved. In
truth, if this went any further I suspected that even
the poor chambermaid might not escape this fate.

"Am I to understand that you are challenging me, sir?" whispered Sandy, his eyes afire. He was already unbuttoning his coat.

"I say, this has gone entirely too far!" I exclaimed, taking Sandy by the arm. "I demand that you..."

I did not finish my sentence, for just then, at the end of the hallway, appeared that most imposing and unwelcome of characters, especially when one is intoxicated: the constable. He was accompanied by a young man, obviously in the employ of the inn. No doubt it was he who was sent to fetch the law, and, unsurprisingly, rather than return to his duties he lingered at the end of the hall to see what would happen next.

"So, what seems to be the trouble here, Jacob?" The constable addressed the proprietor, but stared as us.

"If he says that we have not paid for our room it is a blatant falsehood!" injected Sandy before the old man could speak. "It is there, upon the floor!" He pointed to the money, for emphasis. "The scallywag can bend down to pick it up!" Ignoring this, the landlord angrily expressed his complaints.

"They're creatin' a disturbance! And attemp'in' to leave the grounds with hotel property!"

As the shouting began I stole a glance behind us and noticed that the now-forgotten chambermaid was hard at work, furtively wiping away the odd symbols which had triggered this absurd situation. She spied me spying her and took great pains not to meet my gaze as she finished her work. Curiouser and curiouser.

"Do you mean this?" Sandy continued, producing the note that he had scribbled the symbols upon.

"Yes!" cried the proprietor, pointing with both hands and all but leaping for joy, as if Sandy had been caught red-handed at some criminal enterprise. "That's it, constable! That is the property of this establishment and these young men intended to make off with it on their person! I demand its return!"

The constable stared at the paper for a moment, then his eyes appeared to glaze over and he seemed to go very, very far away. His sigh, a moment later, would be deemed theatrical had it not clearly come from a place of such utter sincerity.

"This." The constable said. "*This* is why you summoned me here? The 'theft' of a single sheet of paper? Really, Jacob..."

"There are important instructions for my employees, written on that very sheet...!"

"'*Furst,* this word is spelled incorrectly, *cleen,* also spelled incorrectly, *all the bedsheets...*'" Sandy began, reading with great gusto. The constable held up his hands, his face red with anger and frustration. Sandy, for once, saw the wisdom in not persisting. The landlord also fell silent. At the end of the hall, the young man who had fetched the constable peeped around the corner, smirking. The constable took a deep breath, held it, slowly let it out, and then addressed us.

"You are from the college, I assume?" he asked.

"Yes," I told him.

"And both parties agree that your bill, at least, has been satisfactorily settled by the money lying here, on the floor?"

"Yes," interjected Sandy, allowing a tone of superiority to creep into his voice. The constable turned to the landlord.

"Yes," the old man hesitantly agreed.

"Then please," said the constable with great patience, "return that fool slip of paper to this man and be on your way."

"Very well," said Sandy. "But I demand the right to tear my own notes, clearly written in my hand, from the bottom so that I may take them with me!"

"No! No!" shouted the landlord. "Destroying my personal property! I shall press changes! Constable!" The constable, gritting his teeth, had clearly had enough.

"Just give him the entire sheet, immediately! I have had my fill of this nonsense!"

"But-" Sandy began before I drove my elbow, with some force, into his ribs. The landlord was beaming now, his outstretched hand like the grasping claw of a bird. At that moment, I hated him his victory, and was half tempted to propose that we run for it. But to his credit Sandy is usually one step ahead of everyone, and his face suddenly lit up. Clearly he'd had an epiphany.

"Very well," he agreed. "One moment." Pulling the small pencil from his suit-coat pocket, he quickly copied the runes down on the cuff of his shirt.

"He can't do that!" the landlord cried. "Constable, that is proprietary information...!"

"Enough!" screamed the constable at the old man as Sandy crammed the paper into his hand. "Do you propose I seize this young man's shirt now? Your business will not be torn asunder if some fool students know what brand of soap your maids use to wash the sheets!" He turned on us. "Begone, the both of you! I don't want to see you near this establishment again!"

"Yes, sir!" we said in unison, immediately taking our leave. And the smile Sandy gave the landlord at that moment... It was all I could do to hold my laughter until we were well out of earshot of the constable, who was still dressing the old man down for calling him out on such a trivial, absurd matter.

"Oh, Sandy!" I managed between guffaws. "With you it is always an adventure!"

Of course, this is Sandford Bernard Harding III, of the Boston Hardings, of which I am speaking, so this was hardly the end of it.

"What could they *mean?*" he asked me, rhetorically, again and again over the next several days. My frivolous responses, such as "Perhaps the interlocking squares represent a tenant who leaves the room untidy!" were met with disapproving frowns, and Sandy continued to obsess over the odd markings, until, finally, he decided to seek enlightenment at the student library, giving me a much needed reprieve from his obsession and finally allowing me to get back to my studies. Peace thus reigned in our tiny little dorm room for the better part of a week, though I knew it was not to last, for Sandy was certainly up to something. He was almost entirely absent during normal waking hours, darted into and out of his classes just long enough for his presence to be noted, and crept in late in the evening, sometimes so late that it was technically morning, bleary-eyed and collapsing into bed like a man who has spent a day at hard labour. While curious, I mentally shrugged my shoulders at these goings-on. Whatever mischief he was engaged in, I'd learn the details soon enough, likely via a personal visit from the dean. I sighed at the thought of this, yet smiled at the same time. There was never a dull moment when Sandford Harding was your mate.

As previously stated, this state of affairs lasted for quite near a week, until finally, inevitably, the peace was broken in that unnecessarily dramatic manner so typical of Sandford. In the wee hours of the morning my peaceful slumber was rudely interrupted when Sandy suddenly burst into the room, lit the lamp and began waving a sheath of papers in my face – notes, apparently – all the while dancing a little jig and shouting "I've done it! I've done it!"

"Done what?" I hesitatingly asked, already dreading where this might be going.

"Look!" exclaimed Sandy, shoving his papers into my face. "It took the most diligent research, but I've finally deciphered three of the symbols Old Landlord painted on our door! Would you like to know what they are? You'll never believe it, Blake! Would you like to know?"

"If I won't believe it, there's no need for me to know," I replied blearily, turning over and pulling the blankets over my head in what I hoped would be an unmistakable indication that I was not in the least bit interested and did not wish to be further disturbed at such an ungodly hour. But Sandy was undeterred.

"The first one," he began, pacing heavily back and forth across the room (as he was wont to do when he was excited), "was easy. See?" He held the paper up, and I could almost sense him standing there, impatiently, until I acquiesced, sat up, and looked at the hand-drawn marking.

"The man is Jewish?" I asked, still half asleep.

"What?" Sandy double-checked the sheet to assure himself that he held up the right one. "No, you ninny, it's not the Star of David. Look closer."

I did as he bade. What I saw was a five-pointed star, one point facing downwards, contained within a circle. I looked to Sandy for an explanation.

"It's a pentagram!" he exclaimed gleefully. "Or, to be more precise, an *inverted* pentagram. Blake, it is the sign of the Devil!"

"I've no doubt we *were* devils that night," I responded dryly. "A fine editorial on our behaviour. Now are you satisfied, or will you be pursuing a case for libel?"

"Blake, you fool!" Sandy exclaimed, irritated now. "If you will recall, every door in that hallway contained some manner of markings. Oh, if only I had recorded them all!" It was clear that he would not let me rest until he had spoken his piece, so, accepting this, I sat up and waited for Sandy to continue. "That's more like it," he said, satisfied with my feigned interest. "Now," he continued, "there were four symbols on our door, and besides the one I've just shown you I've managed to identify two more. Are you ready?" Sighing heavily, I nodded. Sandy produced a second sheet of paper, on which he had drawn two interlocking squares, forming a smaller, third square between them. Inside one of the larger squares was a squiggly vertical line. "This symbol," Sandy said with much pride, "was the most difficult and obscure, but apparently it is an unfathomably ancient symbol representing a meeting, or gathering..." here he paused dramatically "...one that is to be held in secret!" It was all too much. I decided to have some fun with him.

"Did your research suggest *how* ancient this mark might be?" I asked him with the utmost seriousness. He faltered for a moment.

"Why, thousands of years! Perhaps tens of thousands!"

"But you said it was an 'unfathomably' ancient symbol, and I can certainly wrap my head around the concept of something that is, at best, tens of thousands of years old. Why, the dinosaurs are thought to be many millions of years old, and I was reading about them just the other day, my credulity not in the least bit strained."

"Well, that... I mean..." Sandy blustered.

"And furthermore," I continued, quite enjoying myself now, "what use would one have for a mark indicating a secret gathering? After all, employing such a mark would inevitably give away the secret!" By now my smile had given me away, and Sandy threw his notes to the floor in disgust.

"You make light of me, sir! But I assure you that this is no jest! The third marking was the symbol for Saturday, to-morrow, and I have no doubt of what I have uncovered here! And if you've no wish to accompany me to-morrow night, if you'd rather remain here, alone, smirking with satisfaction at your own great wit, then so be it!"

"Sandy, please," I said, holding up my hands in supplication. "It's just that the hour is late, and you are so earnest. Please, tell me what you believe you've discovered." Sandy snorted at me with derision, but having no one else to share his unique madness with, he deigned to continue.

"Of the four symbols," he began again, "I have deciphered three: 'Meeting' or 'Gathering'; 'Saturday'; and 'The Devil'. I dare say, Blake, I am convinced that I – we –have discovered the location of the next meeting of the infamous Hellfire Club!"

"Corncobs and nonsense!" I snorted, in my surprise employing a phase oft-used by my own, dearly-departed grandmother. "Why, there is no such beast! Those stories are abject foolishness, Grimm's for adults!"

"Or perhaps that is what the Hellfire Club *wishes* us to believe," Sandy said with a crooked, knowing smile.

"Even if there were such an entity," I declared, "dedicated, as the stories say, to debauchery and the worship of the Pit, I suspect their meetings would be dire, boring affairs, chiefly concerned with the election of a new treasurer and whom sold the most pastries at the Devil's bake sale. It is late, Sandy, and I bid thee good night!" I rolled over and again pulled my blanket over my head for emphasis, but Sandford was not to be dissuaded.

"Blake," he continued, as if I had not declared my last on the matter, "this is an unprecedented opportunity! The Hellfire Club! Or, perhaps, some rival organization, attempting to emulate their practices in their own, fiendish manner. Whichever, we must be there, Blake! To witness this thing, to confirm the existence of such an organization, simply for our own illumination... what an adventure!" I sighed, for clearly there would be no more sleep tonight. Resigning myself to my fate, I sat up and dutifully listened to Sandy's plan.

* * *

From ingrained, lifelong habit, my Sunday mornings were spent attending the campus church service, with Sunday afternoon and evening dedicated to my studies. Thus, only Saturday was available to me for any leisure activities I wished to pursue, such as reading on the common or participating in social clubs. Therefore I was loathe to accompany Sandy in his campus-wide treasure hunt for the various and sundry items he was convinced we would need for the evening's proposed adventure. Once Sandy is of a mind there is no stopping him, however, so I had no choice but to assist him in his lunatic campaign. A large chef's knife was commandeered from the kitchen. Holy water was surreptitiously pilfered from the stoup just inside the church, which made a point of accommodating all faiths and therefore made it available to those of the Catholic persuasion. Sandy even managed to acquire, from the storage room beneath the bell tower, a twenty-five foot length of strong, hemp rope. "Why?" I asked, clearly exasperated.

"We may have to scale something," was Sandy's terse reply.

And so it was that instead of retiring to our dorm room after a relaxing day spent reading under a tree, or enjoying the company of a lovely co-ed, the early evening found me standing just outside the campus grounds, "loaded for bear", as the American say. Over the course of the day we had managed to relieve the college and/or various colleagues and associates of two lanterns; a shovel; a pail; two pairs of sturdy leather gloves; the aforementioned knife, holy water, and rope; and a large cloth sack, for our spoils, I supposed, after we robbed Satan himself of every last coin in his purse and the bread in his pantry besides.

"No window-peepers have ever been so well-equipped," I quipped.

"Jest all you like," Sandy replied. "I dare say that we are ready for anything!"

"The madhouse, at the very least," I acquiesced.

Successfully hitching a ride whilst loaded down so much ridiculous paraphernalia was quite out of the question, and besides, truth be told we weren't entirely clear exactly where it was we were going. Inquires had turned up a not single individual who knew the location of our mysterious inn ("Perhaps all of our fellow students are in on it!" I suggested. Sandy was not amused.), so we had no choice but to walk all the way into town and, from there, attempt to retrace our steps from the previous evening. This proved to be no small task, especially encumbered as we were with our "equipment", and I began to feel quite the fool as we roamed aimlessly about the side and back roads of town, shovel dragging, bucket rattling, passing vehicles slowing so that the occupants could stare at the two young men, clearly students, traipsing aimlessly around the outskirts of town whilst weighed down with all the accoutrements necessary to rob a grave or perhaps plant a flower bed. It was, frankly, quite embarrassing.

And would that it had ended here. It would have made a fine, funny story of our college days, one to share over a pint of ale in years to come. Or perhaps it would have served to impress upon the next generation a valuable lesson, being that one should not squander one's time and energy on fool's errands. We were fools, of this I have no doubt, but for that it was not a fool's errand which we had committed ourselves to. No, 'twas the Devil's errand, as the two of us would be learning, soon enough.

The hour was late by the time we determined, by sheer process of elimination, the most likely path that we had followed out of town during our previous misadventure. With nary a word between us, we began to trudge down what could charitably be called a cow path, weighed down by our gratuitous "supplies", weary and short-tempered. As we finally left the town completely behind us we were swathed in darkness. The skeletal branches adorning the trees on either side of the path seemed to reach out, to beckon, and I started in fright when one briefly snagged my knapsack. Above us, the stars were lost in black foliage and entwining limbs that had now taken on a decided sinister bent. I did not like it here, I realized, not only because I was tired and uncomfortable, but because the whole of it, in an instant, felt very, very *wrong* in a way I cannot express. Yet we trudged along, in silence, until the path widened and I found myself thinking that yes, this did indeed look familiar. Then, ahead of us, suddenly discernible, mumbling; human voices now competing with the irregular hum and chirrup of insects that had accompanied us since we'd entered the wood. *I do not want to be here. We should not be here...*

"There," stage-whispered Sandy, the unexpected sound of his voice making me jump. Against the darkness, the slightly darker outline of his hand, extending, index finger pointing to a bend in the road a quarter mile or so distant, and just beyond this, the pale glow of lamplight. "I believe we've found it," he whispered, with no bravado. Entirely forgetting that he could not see me in the darkness, I nodded. We stood there then, in silence, for I know not how long. Minutes? Surely less than a minute, yet it felt like hours before I finally steeled myself and took my next, determined step forward.

Sandy's arm swung out and blocked my path.

"Wait, Blake. You forget that these people may well have had designs on us, having marked the very door behind which we slept with the runes that led us here. I suggest we slip through the trees, come up behind the place, and reconnoitre, rather than present ourselves at their front door." Again I nodded, pointlessly, and together we slipped off our packs and hid our equipment in the high grass beside the road before cautiously stepping into the dense woods beyond.

We were instantly enveloped in utter darkness, a darkness so deep and so black that surely death itself has nothing upon it. Worse, it quickly became evident that it is impossible to move quietly, in the dark, through a thick wood. Snaps, cracks, pops, even a light curse from myself – provoking an exasperated "Shush!" from Sandy – accompanied us the entire way, mocking us, telegraphing our location to any who might be listening. We were fools, damned fools, and surely we would be caught if anyone were on the lookout for a pair of clumsy, gate-crashing oafs.

Fortunately, no one was. For suddenly we found ourselves stepping out of the wood and onto a neatly manicured lawn, the outer wall of the inn only a few yards away. With a care that belied our previous clumsiness, we shrank back into the now-comforting darkness of the trees and waited. There were sounds, we heard them again now, at last, over our measured breathing and the staccato beating of our hearts. Laughter, and the unmistakable sounds of revelry, distinct but muffled. I started in surprise yet again as Sandy gently poked me in the ribs, pointing with his other hand in the direction of a cellar window that glowed with a pale, sickly light. Lying down, we used our elbows to quietly drag ourselves across the lawn until we were able to peek inside.

And what we saw...

What we saw is unprintable. Quite simply, every sin imaginable, save murder, was being committed by the people in that torch-lit room. The sheer depravity of it all was almost overwhelming, as if Hell itself had spilt over and allowed the worst of its inhabitants free rein, for just one night, in the cellar off this – literally – God-forsaken place. I cringed, I gagged, but I found I could not look away, my eyes darting back and forth, to and fro, drinking in every sickening atrocity and then, a moment later, spying another even more vile. I do remember that I spied them both there, the landlord and the chambermaid, engaged with a third party in some blasphemous lust I refuse to describe. I recognized others as well, vaguely, townsfolk I'd seen in passing. No students though, thank providence, and had I spied one of our distinguished faculty members in that abominable place I have little doubt I would have left school immediately, never to return. Next to me, Sandy sniffled, and I realized that he was crying, silently, tears not of sorrow or joy but of... what? Terror? Disgust? I did not ask him then and I never shall. Some things are best left unspoken.

And then, as if someone had toggled a switch, their unholy revelries ceased. They froze, as did my heart for I pictured them, having realized they were being spied upon, suddenly turning, as one... coming for us... Now I was weeping too, but while they did indeed turn almost as one it was not in our direction but in that of the open doorway at the opposite end of the flickering cellar, where, a moment later, an unnaturally large, pitch-black housecat adorned with a collar of sparkling gold appeared. I realized that I was shivering with fear but I continued to watch as the sleek, almost luminescent animal – its eyes reflecting the light of a dozen scattered torches so that it seemed to be looking in every direction at once – strode purposefully towards a smallish golden throne situated at the opposite end of the hall. Gently but deliberately, it leapt onto the throne, where it stretched dramatically in a typically cat-like manner and then sat down on its haunches, staring with what appeared to be great interest at the men and women before it. Men and women who, as if on cue, dropped to their knees and bowed down to this animal, some weeping openly, others whispering strange prayers to themselves, and still others doing things to themselves that I will not recount here. The cat adopted a pleased, half-lidded demeanour, and I could swear that it was actually studying its constituents, examining them, *judging* them. Never in my life had I been so afraid as I was at that moment.

A feeling that increased tenfold when, with a sudden jerk of its head, the black cat looked directly at me.

Time did not seem to stop so much as to... end. Perhaps it had been an unnaturally calm night from the start, I freely admit that I do not readily recall, but I would swear that at that very instant the wind suddenly ceased. The insects and night birds fell silent. Even the air itself, previously so cool and refreshing, was suddenly acrid and felt thick in my lungs. I was dimly aware of Sandy, fumbling about his person beside me, but I was far more aware of the occupants of that cellar, who, one by one, slowly turned in our direction, following the cat's gaze, until every man and woman in that den of vile sin was staring directly at us. Calmly, without alarm, the cat hopped off its throne and padded towards the window, its people parting as it passed, none of them taking their eyes off of us, the interlopers, eyes that burned with a hatred the likes of which I had never before in my life beheld. And then the cat was directly below the window, still staring, its eyes hypnotic, holding me there. I dimly perceived motion, the people in the room moving towards the doorway through which the cat had entered – no doubt coming for us – but I didn't care. The whole of my world was in the large black cat's soporific eyes. Eyes that beckoned. Eyes that danced with all the colours of the rainbow, all the colours *possible,* and more besides. Eyes that promised agonies the likes of which even the damned could not begin to imagine. Yet there I stayed, motionless, obediently awaiting my fate. *This has been preordained,* I told myself. *It is only fitting that...*

Then, abrupt motion beside me, something nearly hitting my face, followed by the sound of shattering glass. Sandy was screaming – gibberish, not words –

and he had kicked in the cellar window. Forcing his arm through the breakage he hurled an uncapped vial at the startled cat, the vial we had earlier filled with holy water. And wherever the liquid touched its fur or flesh a sizzling grey smoke formed, erupting dramatically into the air like gas from a punctured balloon. Screeching horribly, the cat began running in wild circles, panicking its constituents, who pushed and struck and trampled one another in an attempt to stay out of the animal's erratic path. Torches were toppled, oils used in the group's debauchery ignited, clothing ignited, people fell to the floor, and before I realized what was happening it was a conflagration. Chaos reigned; men and women, unable to find the exit in their hysteria, shrieked in fear, frustration, and agony; and yet above them all I could hear that damnable animal squalling and screaming in anger and pain, as if it were both inside my head and outside it, dying in agony in that flaming cellar and trying to tear its way out of my brain simultaneously. Without warning one of the assemblage, somehow come up behind me, grabbed the collar of my shirt. I screamed, tried to fight, but no, it was not one of them, it was Sandy, screaming himself, weeping, dragging me across the lawn and away from the broken window just as the hairy, muscular arm of a man, engulfed in flame, burst through it. He was staring at us and howling like a beast – whether in anger or pain or fear I do not know – and trying to pull himself out, through the window, without success. The blaze was climbing the sides of the building now, licking the roof. Something collapsed inside and plumes of flame blew out the remaining cellar windows with a dull *boom* like distant, heavy artillery. Nothing could have lived through that, nothing, nothing, and yet we ran, ran, though dead branches tore our clothes and rocks bit through my stocking, bloodying my foot (I had somehow lost a shoe), still we ran, through the darkness and into town and on and on and on until, at last, we found ourselves on the school common, the dawn spilling pink over the horizon, where we finally collapsed in the grass, wet, bloodied, but safe at last. Would it not have been grounds for a personal inquiry, I could have slept right there, I think. It would have been a good sleep. A dreamless sleep. The sleep of the just.

Sandy had better write that book. He certainly is not wanting for subject matter now.

Everything You Ever Wanted For a Dollar

That recurring dream, where you stumble across this neat little store full of amazing things but then you can never find it again. Does everyone have that one, or is it just me?

"Hey, let's go in here!"

Smithy frowned as he read the sign: *Everything You Ever Wanted: $1.*

"These places just sell cheap, Chinese crap," he said. "And expired energy drinks."

Bennie was peeping in the window.

"Nah, it doesn't look like a *dollar store* dollar store, more like a junk shop. Wait out here if you want. I'm gonna check it out."

A bell rang as they entered. An actual, physical bell, positioned over the door. Old school.

"Man, lookit this place!"

It was like something out of an old movie. Cluttered in a carefully calculated way, items displayed on oak shelving and tables, the air thick with the scent of polished wood. The kind of place where you might find a book of antediluvian magic, bound in skin – magic that really worked. Or a Gremlin, in its deceptively adorable, Mogwai guise. In fact, there was a Mogwai staring at them from one of the wooden shelves. A plush, circa 1984. That's what ultimately dispelled the illusion – all the toys and pop culture detritus, most of it from well before Smithy's time. Shogun Warriors; Micronauts; sprawling He-Man playsets; 3¾" figures from the 1979 movie *Alien*. Smithy picked up one of the *Alien* figures and examined it. A poor approximation of Veronica Cartwright, in molded plastic. He didn't even know they made action figures based on that movie. He'd read somewhere that they had *planned* to, but parents got all riled up because the movie was a hard R, so the idea was scrapped. Maybe these were new, some sort of nostalgia line. He turned the figure – still in its package – over. Produced 1980. Who knew?

"Holy crap, look at this!"

Bennie was holding a small, loose figure in his hand. A little robot, its round feet nestled in a clear plastic stand to prevent it falling over.

"Doesn't ring any bells," Smithy said, squinting at it. It looked like what might happen if *Star Wars'* BB-8 was run through a garbage disposal.

"It's Old B.O.B., from *The Black Hole*."

Smithy stared at him blankly.

"*The Black Hole*. Disney's answer to *Star Wars*. It kinda flopped – or underperformed, anyway – but they made tons of merch, including action figures. This one was super rare; you could only get it in Canada and I think Italy. *Damn* but I wanted one of these as a kid."

"Why would they release a toy based on a major motion picture in only Canada and Italy?"

"Man, I dunno. But that's the story."

"That item is only one dollar." Neither of them said this.

They turned in the direction of the voice. Smithy expected a gnarled old man, ethnic and aged beyond reason, wreathed in exotic smoke, a long cigarette holder dangling from his mouth. Whatever they purchased he'd warn them, vaguely but ominously, about its potential misuse.

But no, it was just some guy in a sports jacket. Youngish, good hair. From his mannerisms, Smithy guessed him gay.

"Really?" Bennie said. "Because it's loose?"

"Not as loose as me, tiger," Sports Jacket said. Definitely gay. "But no," he quickly went on. "Like the sign says, everything's a dollar."

"*All* of these collectibles are a dollar?" Bennie repeated.

"Well, *each*," Sports Jacket emphasized.

Something caught Smithy's eye, deeper in the store. They had records, and some CDs. He drifted over and started flipping through them. Almost immediately, he found a CD he'd spent years looking for, back when obscure music was his life and he was sure he'd start a band of his own... some day. Recently he'd downloaded the MP3 version in a fit of nostalgia, but he'd only listened to it the once. It belonged to a previous incarnation, a Smithy now inconsequential and mostly forgotten. But what he wouldn't have given for this CD back then.

"What's your minimum credit card purchase?" Bennie was asking.

"Oh, we don't take credit cards. At all. Sorry."

Bennie's face fell. He patted his pockets for change, even though he knew he didn't have any.

"How late are you open?" he asked. There was the slightest hint of panic in his voice.

"We're open whenever you need us," Sports Jacket said. Not really an answer. Sarcasm? Yet he seemed earnest.

"Here," Smithy fished a dollar out of his pocket, change from their movie tickets. "It's all I've got. You're literally breaking me." Bennie, genuinely relieved, gratefully took the crumpled dollar from Smithy and handed it over.

"There's tax..." Sports Jacket said apologetically. Bennie blanched. "You know what, don't worry about it. I'll steal it from the take-a-penny dish." Sports Jacket stepped behind the long, oak counter, popped the drawer of an ancient cash register, and mashed the bill inside. "Nothing for you?" he asked Smithy.

Smithy thought about the CD.

"Naw, I'm good." He grinned. "I guess I'm the man who has everything."

Sports Jacket stared at him, a strange look in his eyes. Judgmental, almost. Yet also pitying.

"Well lucky you," he said.

Smithy's stomach sank, and he couldn't say why.

"C'mon, we gotta go," Bennie said, never taking his eyes off his purchase. "Juanita's expecting me."

Juanita was waiting on the front stoop, sipping an iced tea and vaping. Her jeans were ridiculously tight and Smithy tried, unsuccessfully, not to stare. Juanita leaned more towards adorable than fashion model, but Smithy liked that. She was a lot younger than Bennie, but seemingly devoted and endlessly indulgent of his nonsense. Smithy had long felt Bennie took her for granted.

"Hi, Smithy," she said before she gently lit into

Bennie for being late.

"Sorry hon, but look what I got." He held up his prize.

"What is it?"

"It's Old B.O.B."

"B.Y.O.B.?"

"B.O.B. Old Bob. From *The Black Hole*."

Her look was even blanker than Smithy's had been.

"It's a science fiction movie. From Disney."

"Oh, I know that movie," Juanita said, rolling her eyes. "It's *terrible*."

"Bite your tongue."

"Where did you get it?"

Smithy answered for him.

"Briarkirche Plaza. There's a whole new row of shops behind the movie theater."

"More toys and comics, just what he needs." Juanita winked at Smithy.

"It's more of an antique store," Bennie insisted. "They had stuff you'd like too, hon..."

They did, Smithy realized, and it was strange because this really only registered now that Bennie had mentioned it. Furniture, jewelry, bicycles; they had all sorts of stuff. Why hadn't he noticed when they were actually there? Now the memory of all these wonderful things was crystal clear, so much so that it felt artificial, implanted.

"...and get this: Everything is only a dollar."

"*Mentiras*." Juanita rolled her eyes again.

"It's probably just the action figures that are a dollar," Smithy interjected.

"Be that as it may, I'm going back tomorrow and cleaning them out. Anything I don't want, I'll sell online. I'll make a killing on those vintage, carded

TMNT figures alone."

Smithy didn't recall there being any TMNT figures.

"Oh, *papi*, you're as dumb as you are handsome," Juanita said. "It's the classic bait and switch. I guarantee, you go back there and won't nothing be no dollar."

"Bet on it?" Bennie said, extending his hand.

Instead of taking his hand, she crossed her arms.

"How much you wanna bet?" she asked, suspicious.

"A dollar," he grinned.

She almost laughed, and this irritated her, so she started yelling at him in Spanish, and he started yelling back in English, with the few Spanish swear words he knew peppered in. It wasn't a proper fight, just something they did, but it went on all night, and well into the morning.

And in the end all their back-and-forth about *Everything You Ever Wanted: $1* came to naught, because when Bennie returned the next day, cash in hand, the store was gone.

"It probably went out of business," Smithy suggested.

"No, you don't understand. It was *gone*. Like there was never a store there at all."

"All those storefronts look the same when the signs come down." Smithy had an epiphany. "Shit, we probably stumbled into an unannounced going-out-of-business sale. *That's* why everything was a dollar."

"That register jockey didn't *say* they were going out of business," Bennie pouted. "He was probably keeping it on the down-low so he could save all the best stuff for himself, or sell it to his friends."

"Or maybe he was the owner and realized that he was better off putting the stuff up for auction."

"Shit. I feel like I found a hundred dollar bill on the ground and the wind whipped it away before I could pick it up."

"Well, at least you got Old Bob."

"Fuck Old Bob."

Months passed, and Smithy forgot all about *Everything You Ever Wanted*. They were grey, lonely months – the days longer than the years – but they always had been and when he was aware of his malaise it was as someone watching another person from a distance. And then, on a particularly beige morning, he looked up and saw the sign. *Everything You Ever Wanted: $1*. But he wasn't anywhere near Briarkirche. In fact, he was downtown, south of the loop. It must have moved. Mystery solved. He looked forward to telling Bennie. Although he hadn't seen Bennie much lately.

Smithy never made the decision to actually go into the store, but somehow, suddenly, he was stepping through the door, the bell ringing lightly. The same clerk was working. Different sports jacket, though, this one tastefully flamboyant. "Came back for that CD?" he asked, as if Smithy had just been there yesterday.

"Er," said Smithy. He felt off, discombobulated.

"Did your friend enjoy his little robot?" the clerk continued. He said this with a bit of a smirk.

"Yeah, yeah," Smithy said, composing himself. "He tried to come back, but he couldn't find you. He wanted some more of your old toys."

"Well, there are things we want, and things we *need*."

Maybe I will get that CD, Smithy thought. *It might cheer me up.*

"Fleetingly," Sports Jacket said.

"What?"

"Buying that CD might cheer you up, but only fleetingly." A pause. "If you don't mind my saying."

Had he spoken aloud? Smithy didn't think that he had spoken the thought aloud. In fact, he was sure he hadn't. Suddenly he was frightened, like a man who knows he's being stalked by an unseen animal.

"Did you...?" he managed.

"Did I what?" asked Sports Jacket.

Smithy stared at him, thought at him as hard as he could: *Your jacket is ugly.*

Sports Jacket simply stared back.

"I should probably go," Smithy said, turning towards the door.

"Are you lonely?" Sports Jacket asked.

Smithy froze. Was this guy hitting on him?

"I'm straight," he said carefully.

"Sorry about your luck." The clerk waited a beat before continuing. "We don't just sell physical goods, you know, is what I'm saying." This latter was delivered conspiratorially, as if he were suggesting something illegal. Smithy turned and stared at him.

"I'm not offering to suck you off if that's what you're thinking," Sports Jacket said, rolling his eyes. He gestured. Follow me. Smithy did.

Instantly, it seemed, they were in another part of the store, staring at a wall of rickety wooden shelving. Near-opaque bottles of colored glass lined these shelves, embossed text identifying their contents. No, not their contents. Abstractions. FREEDOM. HOPE. SUCCESS. Smithy picked one up. DA'AT. He didn't even know what that word meant. Something swirled around inside, just barely discernible through the dark glass. He reached for the stopper but Sports Jacket gently guided his hand away. "You open it, you bought it," he explained. "And there's only one per customer. He relieved Smithy of DA'AT and carefully put it back on the shelf. "I think this is the one you're looking for." He passed a dark, blood-red jar to Smithy. TRUE LOVE.

"Come on..." Smithy said. But he couldn't tear his eyes away from the object in his hand. The swirling whatsit inside was hypnotizing. Like watching a lava lamp. "So what, do I pour this in her drink or something?"

"You're thinking of Spanish Fly." Sports Jacket was joking, but his tone was polite, reverent. "This, you just have to open. Let it out and it does its thing."

"Like burning sage to cleanse a house," Smithy said. "My grandmother used to do that..." His thoughts were jumbled, his mind drifting.

"Something like that, yes. Something very much like that."

Smithy shook his head as if awakening from a dream. He was standing at the front counter, a dollar in one hand, the blood-red jar in the other. "Tax," Sports Jacket reminded him. He dug into a pocket and found seven cents, staring at his purchase all the while, feeling more than a little foolish. But hey, it was only a dollar, and if nothing else it was an amusing novelty, the centerpiece to hang a terrific story on later. Yeah, yeah, this was all right.

"I suppose it comes with a warning?" he smiled. "Not to misuse the arcane forces within and all that?"

"Meh," Sports Jacket shrugged. "Do you need a receipt?"

It was over a week before Smithy actually opened the jar. Mostly because he was concerned that the mesmerizing swirling effect would be compromised. And, much to his regret, it was, whatever gas or substance that had been inside quickly escaping and dissipating into the air. Oh well. It had been, he reminded himself, only a dollar. In fact, it seemed a lot less impressive now; just a colorful glass jar. You could buy something similar at any Target. Within days it was relegated to the cabinet underneath the sink, where he kept the cleaning supplies. He'd all but forgotten about the jar by the time it happened.

It started with a phone call. Juanita. This was unusual. If asked, Smithy would have counted Juanita among his friends, but in reality she was more of a friend-in-law, with Bennie as the connective tissue. Strange that she would call him, would subsequently meet him for coffee without Bennie in tow. But then Bennie, so it seemed, was the problem. "I wasn't sure who else to talk to." "You know him better than anyone."

"It's just not working."

"I'm not happy. *We're* not happy."

"You're a really good listener."

Coffee, again.

Dinner.

The age-old story. Predictable. Inevitable.

She moved in four months later.

Bennie, after an intense but short-lived campaign against the both of them on various social media platforms, cut any and all ties. But Smithy didn't care. Because this wasn't an opportunistic pairing, nor one of convenience, nor a case of any port in a storm.

They were in love.

And it was glorious.

"I'll be damned," Bennie said.

The bell over the door dinged as he stepped in. Same clerk. Different sports jacket though.

"Thought you went out of business. Just moved, huh?"

"You bought... that little robot," Sports Jacket said.

"You remembered."

"Like an elephant."

Bennie perused the shelves. They didn't have so many vintage toys at this new location.

"Back for some more nostalgia?" Sports Jacket asked perfunctorily. He'd made a show of turning his attention to some paperwork.

Bennie grunted noncommittally.

"Bad day?" Sports Jacket asked.

"Bad life."

Sports Jacket set aside his paperwork and locked eyes with Bennie.

"We might have something for that," he said conspiratorially.

It seemed as if they were instantaneously in another part of the store. Deeper. Before them: ornate glass jars with embossed text, lined up on distressed wooden shelves. Sports Jacket selected one, handed it over.

"I think this is what you're looking for."
Bennie ran a thumb over the raised glass letters.
REVENGE, they read.

Dog Days

"Why can't you just admit that we're lost?" Gwen snapped at him. Paul narrowed his eyes and, without a word, hit the accelerator so hard that she actually let out a little gasp. The Mustang tore down the old dirt road, throwing up a hazy cloud of brown dust behind them. The endless fields of wheat flanking the road smeared into a golden blur, the shocks bounced wildly in protest, and she half-expected the next bump to launch them into the air like a co-ed Dukes of Hazzard. "What are you *doing?*" she screamed.

"I'm admitting it, okay? I'm admitting we're lost. So the smart thing to do is to find someplace to ask directions as quickly as possible, right?"

"Well there's no point in getting us killed!" She was in full bitch mode now, Paul could tell by the way her eyes were sparkling. They sparkled in much the same way when she was excited, or horny, but he knew she enjoyed a good fight as much as a good fuck. Maybe more. He slowed down.

"Look, I'm sorry," he said. "I'm just a little pissed off right now."

"You're pissed off because your male ego can't accept the fact that you fucked up." She tried to toss her hair back in a gesture of finality: *I've had the last word.* It wouldn't cooperate though. Never should've cut it short, she thought.

"The GPS is what's fucked up," Paul mumbled, and his tone told her to drop it. She couldn't help smirking though, so she took a sudden interest in the landscape to keep him from noticing.

A quarter hour passed before either of them spoke again. Paul was driving at a reasonable speed again, but given the condition of the road he didn't have much choice; even creeping along at well below the posted limit they'd bottomed out more than once. Somehow they still managed to churn up a cloud of dust though, so much so that Gwen found herself rolling up her window, despite the oppressive heat. The Mustang's AC had given out a week ago; Paul had promised to get it fixed but, typical male, he had never gotten around to it. Of course, how could he have know that the cool, breezy seventies that had dominated the first half of the summer would be supplanted by days of this scorching, humid ninety-five? Global warming indeed, she thought, wiping sweat from her upper lip. And now they were lost on some godforsaken cow path, hours late...

"Oh shit."

"What?" she asked, snapping out of her reverie. Paul looked concerned. Then she felt the car shudder.

"Come on," he mumbled, ignoring her. The dash suddenly lit up with an infuriatingly vague orange legend that suggested they "SERVICE ENGINE SOON". The car shuddered again and stalled. "Shit!" Paul managed to growl and sigh simultaneously. He turned off the key.

"What's wrong?" she asked again.

"God only knows." He climbed out of the car and pulled the hood release, setting his glasses on the roof before he opened it. He stepped back quickly to escape the heat that billowed forth. "Damn that's hot." Gwen slid out and joined him.

"Prognosis, Doctor?" Paul shook his head.

"Need to let it cool down for a few minutes before I try to look at it." A rivulet of sweat rolled down his face and he wiped it away with no little annoyance. "*Damn* is it hot."

"Said the idiot who wore long pants." He gritted his teeth and for an instant she thought he was going to turn on her, but her smile was so mischievous that all he could do was smile back.

"You're a bitch."

"Yup." He pulled her close and kissed her, but she pushed him away. "Don't touch me when I'm gross." She was surprised to see a pout forming on his face. What, did he want to do it right here in the road? She decided to redirect his attention. "Big man fix car?" she cooed. He grunted like a caveman and turned his attention back to the engine. Gwen left him to it and decided to look for some shade, not that she held out much hope of finding any. It was damn unpleasant out here in the sun, but she knew it would be even worse in the car – the thing threw heat like a bitch. Oh well, she thought, wandering away from the car, she needed a cigarette anyway.

Gwen walked a good hundred yards down the road and topped a small hill before she stopped to light up. That alone had her sweating like a pig, and she wasn't happy about it. It was too hot to smoke, really, but she needed the fix. Glancing around there was still nothing to see for miles, nothing but wheat wheat wheat. Who ate all that cereal, anyway? she wondered. Maybe they sold it to the Russians. But then she saw something else, something that *did* make her happy. She turned to call out to Paul when the hand fell hard on her shoulder. She started and spun around, dropping her Marlboro in the process, but it was only her husband.

"God, sorry," he said, his eyes laughing at her. He had put his glasses back on and was carrying a thin strip of metal in one hand. Sweat trickled down his brow.

"Did you figure out what was wrong?" she asked, unconsciously pulling out another cigarette. Paul wobbled the metal strip at her.

"Bone dry," he said. She lit her smoke while giving him a look that said *I haven't the foggiest idea what you're talking about*. He explained. "The oil, dear. We have no oil."

"No oil? Where did it all go?" She took a drag.

"No idea. I'm guessing we busted up the oil pan when we kept bottoming out back there." *We*, Gwen noted. Because he had been driving. If she'd been driving it would have been *you*. Her fault. Paul looked back in the direction of their car and beyond, as if he expected to see a trail of oil snaking back along their path like bread crumbs in a fairy tale.

"Well, I think *we're* saved, Mr. Fixit. Have a look-see over yonder." Paul followed her gaze and finally saw it: a ramshackle building flanked by gas pumps and sporting a battered, weather-beaten sign that was just-barely legible: "Sam & Ed's Gas 'n' Groceries". The place was so run-down that, driving past, at a reasonable speed, you'd likely take it to be abandoned. But no, there were definitely two people sitting out front, motionless, like sentries.

"Gwen," Paul smiled, "Sometimes I love you."

The couple walked down the hill arm-in-arm, and within seconds they were sweating profusely. "It's too hot to be in love," Paul mumbled. As they neared the building they got a better look at the two people manning the station: two men, apparently well into their seventies, both wearing overalls and hats despite the oppressive heat. They sat in cheap, aluminum lawn chairs, and watched the approaching couple with no particular interest, though they never took their eyes off them, either. Gwen suddenly grabbed Paul's arm with her free hand.

"Paul, look. They've got guns."

Indeed, a shotgun lay across each man's lap. Paul froze and Gwen followed suit. They all stared at each other for a moment, until finally one of the old men lifted a hand in a half wave. Paul relaxed, and waved in return.

"They seem friendly enough," he said. "What, did you think they were going to shoot us?" He called out, "Afternoon!"

"That it is," replied one of the men. "Car trouble? Or you folks out for a really long stroll?"

"As a matter of fact, we seem to have run out of oil," Paul answered. They were only a few feet away from the old men now, and Gwen could see their eyes darting back and forth, at them and then past them. She fought the urge to turn around and see if something were, in fact bearing down on them. At the same time though, both men were nodding in agreement with Paul's diagnosis, as if they'd examined the car themselves and had already confirmed what he was saying.

"Well, we can help you out there, I think, right Ed?" the man who had been doing all the talking concluded. The other fellow – Ed, apparently – politely nodded before spitting into a dip cup that sat on the ground between his feet. "Why don't you amble on inside and get some oil for these folks?" Ed rose, taking his shotgun (a **double-barreled** shotgun, Gwen noted) with him. He shuffled into the store, glancing left and right before he did so. Gwen found herself swallowing nervously – they seemed so watchful, so vigilant. The other man, (who was probably Sam, Gwen decided), was still talking to Paul, but his eyes continued to dart this way and that, endlessly looking for something, something. God, didn't Paul *notice?* Men were so *blind* sometimes!

"...real life-saver," Paul was finishing. He seemed to have run out of things to say, so he kind of shuffled his feet for a minute. Oh oh, Gwen thought, he's going to say something dumb. Paul couldn't bear the sound of silence, and if no one else was talking he always felt this compulsive need to fill the void. *Not now,* she thought at him, for she was very afraid of saying something wrong to these men. They seemed so skittish, maybe even a little nuts. And they had guns. She spoke before Paul could.

"Do you have a phone?" she asked. "I really want to call my mother and let her know we're okay." She could sense Paul's questioning look – they both had cell phones on them, and Gwen's mother had passed away when she was a child.

"Sorry, Ma'am, but ain't had phone service out here since..." he thought for a moment, and then called over his shoulder, "Hey, Ed! When we'd last git the tellyphone out here?"

"Seventy-six!" came Ed's voice from within the store.

"Ya old fart! It was seventy-nine! I remember." The man who was probably Sam smiled an apologetic smile at Gwen and confirmed this with a nod. "Seventy-nine."

"Oh, well, thanks." Ed was shuffling out of the building now, holding a plastic bag containing five quarts of oil in one hand and his shotgun in the other. He held the gun so that he could aim and fire at a moment's notice, Gwen realized, and this frightened her. She wanted nothing more than to be away from this place, and as quickly as possible. But Paul seemed oblivious to the fact that anything was out of the ordinary here, so much so that she wanted to scream. And then her husband did something that made any potential scream die in her throat.

"Say," he said, "what's with the artillery? You expecting a hold-up?"

This is it, she thought, *they're going to shoot us, right here in broad-yokel-daylight. Shoot us and use us as fertilizer for these endless fields of wheat. Why did you have to say anything, Paul? Why, why, why?* But probably-Sam just shrugged as Ed handed over the bag.

"Dog days," he replied.

"I hear you," Paul said, wiping his brow with his wrist. Gwen's legs felt like jelly. "Listen," Paul went on, "we could probably use some gas too..."

"Sir," said probably-Sam, "them pumps ain't worked since, what Ed? Eighty-two?" Ed, seated again, nodded in agreement.

"Eighty-two," he confirmed, spitting into his cup.

Paul just stood there for a moment, and Gwen half-expected him to say something else stupid ("You guys ever kill anyone before?"), but he only replied "So, what do we owe you?"

"Make it twenty, even."

"Let me see if I have two tens," Paul said, fumbling through his wallet.

"Oh, we take credit cards," said Ed.

"Those two were *weird*." Gwen was smoking another cigarette while Paul poured the oil into the engine.

"I believe the word is *eccentric*," he said, closing the hood.

"No," she snapped, "rich people are *eccentric*. Those two were certifiable. I'm surprised we didn't end up hanging on meat hooks."

"Me, maybe. You, I'm sure they would have raped for days, before selling you to the hill people." She glared at him. "Um, I believe that's a compliment," he added, grinning like an asshole.

"Stupid fucking prick," she snarled.

"Honestly, Gwen, they were just a couple of senile old coots." He indicated the ground at her feet. "When did you become a chain smoker?"

"Huh?" She glanced down and saw two butts, making the cigarette in her hand her third in the last few minutes. She looked back at Paul. "I'm sorry, but they really *scared* me. I thought they were gonna shoot you when you asked about their guns! And what did that guy mean by 'dog days' anyway? What, do they go on shotgun rampages whenever it gets hot around here?" She took a final puff and dropped the spent cigarette, catching herself before she took out a fourth.

"He meant," Paul said, slipping behind the wheel, "that people go a little crazy when it gets this hot. Remember those psychology classes you took?" Gwen nodded as she slid into the car. "I'm sure they just want to be prepared in case some thugs show up and try to rob the place. I mean, they are all alone out here, half past the middle of no place...."

"With no phone service," she added, seeing his point. She was starting to feel a little sheepish; probably she had been overreacting. Still, she decided, if Paul teased her about this later, no sex for a month. They cruised past Ed and probably-Sam and Paul lifted his hand in a wave. Both men waved back, and then they were lost in the roiling clouds of dust.

Five minutes later the dirt road became a gravel road, and ten minutes after that, they were driving on honest-to-god pavement. Gwen stole a look out the back window and frowned. "Oh, lover boy? If anyone's following us, we're leaving a pretty clear trail for them."

"Shit," Paul said, glancing in the rear-view. "I guess we do have a leak."

"What now?" asked Gwen. She hated herself for wanting another cigarette.

"Now," he responded, indicating the first proper exit ramp they'd seen for hours, rapidly coming up on their left, "we go *there*."

"MYER'S GAP" promised the sign.

"Hallelujah, can I have a witness?" said Gwen, as Paul took the exit.

Less than a minute later the road widened and the wheat fell away, disgorging a small, inexplicably charmless town of the type that only seem to exist in the Midwest. There was a single intersection, regulated by a lonely traffic light that blinked an endless, weary red, as if even it were affected by the oppressive heat. A few small businesses lined the streets, but there was no quaint barber shop complete with classic barber pole, no old-fashioned candy store or charming curio shop. Instead, the most visible businesses were a nondescript diner (if the sign out front was to be believed, it was called, simply, "Food"), and a bar with a neon "Colders 29°" sign hanging in the window. And not far down the road, just what they were looking for: a service station sporting sparkling clean pumps, free air, lotto, DVD rentals, "Beer At State Minimum!", and even a Subway sandwich franchise. "I see the real world has conquered Myer's Gap," Paul smiled. They pulled into the lot and Paul cut the engine just in time to hear a bell "Ding!" inside. They waited several seconds, but no one responded. "I'll let 'em know we need more than just gas," Paul said, climbing out of the car.

Gwen leaned out her window. "We'll pay out the ass to get work done at a little place like this!" she said.

"Well we can't drive it as is. Christ, Gwen, there's a friggin' *puddle* under the car." He looked at the oil pooling up underneath the vehicle in disgust. "I've got my credit cards. If those crazy old guys down the road take them, I'm sure this place does." Gwen sighed and resisted the urge to pull out another smoke. She looked absently up and down the street and for the first time noticed how tightly closed up everything was. They must all have their air conditioning on, she thought. Paul was already walking back towards the car.

"What's up?" she asked.

"Closed," he answered, looking up and down the street himself. He didn't see a single soul, just a German shepherd trotting purposefully down the sidewalk in their general direction, it's tongue hanging out, panting from the heat. "Closed on a Wednesday afternoon. Weird, huh?"

"I doubt they get much business on weekdays. Everyone's probably at the bar keeping cool."

"Hang on." He jogged across the street and tried the door to the bar. It was locked. Shielding his eyes from the sun, he looked inside. The place was empty, but he could clearly see the large, hand-lettered sign hanging behind the bar. **"CLOSED FOR DOG DAYS"** it read. He communicated this to Gwen.

"Huh. Maybe they *don't* have air conditioning," she said aloud.

"What?" Paul called over his shoulder.

"Nothing," she answered, but he wasn't even listening anymore as he made his way up the street, trying door after door. All were locked up tight. Gwen sighed again and decided to give in to her nicotine craving, but just then something caught her eye. It was the German shepherd Paul had noticed earlier – hackles raised, mouth twisted in a snarl, charging full-bore towards her husband! Gwen gasped, began to cry out to him, but, inexplicably, her husband was already screaming.

Gwen spun around in her seat to see what was happening and realized that Paul wasn't even looking at the charging German shepherd – instead, he seemed to be doing some sort of crazy dance, yelling and cursing as he hopped around on one leg and shook the other one like he was trying to make it fall off. And then Gwen realized what was going on – one of those little Mexican dogs, like the one that used to shill for Taco Bell, had attached itself to his leg and was tearing at his pants and shin. "What the hell?" he was yelling. "Little bastard!" It would have been comical, if it weren't for...

"Paul!" she screamed. "Look out!" She launched herself out of the car just as he looked up to see the German shepherd launching itself at his throat. He instinctively threw up an arm, which probably prevented him from being killed outright, but the shepherd clamped down on on his upper arm hard and began to shake, just like Gwen had seen police dogs do on television. The people on TV always had thick padding wrapped around their arms though, Paul did not. Blood sprayed from his inner arm. Gwen was across the street now, right on top of them, and, snatching up the first thing she saw, she grabbed the scruff of the German shepherd's neck with one hand and began to bash it over the head with the object in the other. It whined once but refused to loosen its grip, so she continued to pummel it, over and over, her screams mixing with Paul's until she couldn't tell the difference anymore. Suddenly there was a nauseating *crunch* and her hands were drenched first in blood, and then in something thicker. (Brains?) The big dog finally let go and collapsed to the sidewalk. Gwendolyn dropped her weapon, only now realizing that it was a discarded beer bottle. She collapsed to her knees, fighting the urge to vomit. Paul continued to thrash about, and she realized that the little Taco Bell dog was still savagely gnawing on his leg. Furious, she pulled it free and hurled it down the street, where it landed head-first on the concrete with an audible *Crack!* Dead? No, not quite. It stood up, snarling. But something was wrong, because all it did was snap at the air and stumble around in a drunken circle.

Paul was clutching his arm to his chest and, dear God, the blood wasn't just oozing out, it was *spurting* out. They had to get to a hospital. They... "Holy fuck," he gasped, and he wasn't even looking at his arm, the blood... he was looking over her shoulder. Slowly she turned, and she was sure she felt her heart skip a beat.

The road was full of dogs, dogs of all shapes and sizes. Little dogs, big dogs, mongrels, purebreds, a few wearing collars, most not. Collies, poodles, rottweilers, pit bulls, dachshunds, even a mutt that looked like the lovable star of those old "Benji" movies. But none of these dogs looked lovable. And more and more were joining their ranks, slipping out from behind dumpsters and underneath cars. Gwen saw one exit a building through a doggy door to join them. A low growl seemed to ripple through the pack, but they weren't advancing. They were merely... gathering.

Paul was on his feet now, pushing something into her hands. "Keys," he gasped. "You have to take the keys. I can't drive like this." She took his good arm *(God, there was so much blood)* and slowly began to sidle across the street towards the Mustang, keeping her eyes fixed on the growing horde before them.

"Don't run, Paul," she stage-whispered. "Whatever you do don't run..." They were halfway home when he nudged her with his elbow and cocked his head down the street in the opposite direction.

Dogs were gathering there too. They might get to the car, but once inside, they were trapped. "We'll just have to drive right through them," Gwen said, narrowing her eyes. They were almost there now, just a few more feet...

Then as one, the animals charged.

"Go!" she screamed, pushing Paul towards the car. He seemed disoriented, stumbling and falling against the door. She had to reach around and under him to get to the handle, pushing him aside so that she could open it. Paul fell to his knees, and she found herself grabbing him by the shirt collar and half-dragging, half-pushing him into the vehicle. He managed to drag himself across to the passenger side, and she fell in and pulled the door shut just in time for a rottweiler, running full-tilt, to smash head-first into it. The dog recovered immediately and tried to force its head through the window as Gwen rolled it up. The entire car was surrounded by dogs now. An Afghan hound was on its hind legs, barking and snapping at Paul through his closed window. Several medium-sized mutts had clambered onto the hood, and a few even climbed onto the roof. A Labrador Retriever repeatedly and savagely assaulted one of the front tires. Gwen keyed the ignition, but instead of starting smoothly the car lurched forward, pinning the Lab under the wheel it had been attacking, where it howled in agony. There was a horrific *BANG!,* followed by the Tommy gun staccato of a thrown rod. The OIL and SERVICE ENGINE SOON lights came on. Her stomach sank. "Oil..." she muttered.

"We... we need to..." Paul whispered. He sounded like he was going to pass out. Gwen screamed as a

Saint Bernard suddenly threw itself against the driver-side window, spiderwebbing it into thousands of tiny glass diamonds. Paul took his wife's hand, smearing it with blood. "I really do love you," he managed before he slipped into unconsciousness. Tears were streaming down her face.

"I love you too," she said, leaning over to kiss his forehead. The car hitched forward one final time, and died.

The two old men who had sold Paul and Gwen the oil, Ed and, yes, Sam, were still sitting in their aluminum lawn chairs as the sun slowly sank beneath the horizon, staining the sky a bright, arterial red. There hadn't been another customer all day, not that this was unusual. "Getting' late," observed Ed. It was the first time he had spoken in hours.

"Yup," confirmed Sam. "Still damn hot though."

"That it is, that it is," agreed Ed. "Dog days of summer." Sam thought about that phrase for a minute.

"Say," he ventured, "you think them strangers knew what I meant when I told 'em why we need to carry guns this time of year?" Ed pondered this for a while.

"No tellin', I guess," he finally said, before spitting another stream of tobacco juice into the cup at his feet.

The Carved One

"She's beautiful."

The elderly proprietor's face fell, but he quickly recovered.

"That one, very special. Very special indeed."

"Is it one of yours?" Derek asked.

"I carve all of my puppets, all of my dolls. They are... my family." The old man shrugged. Having admitted too much, he felt foolish.

"And they're all based on real people, you say?"

"Oh yes. In the old days, people sat for me all the time. Some likenesses are better than others, of course. The newer figures, not as good." He shrugged again. "Old hands."

Derek picked the doll up to examine it more closely.

"So who is this one based on? A supermodel?"

"My daughter, Rebecca. That is her real hair, you know."

"Really?" Derek ran his fingers through the doll's silky blonde hair. Kinda freaky. Unbidden, lampshades made of human skin came to mind.

"The eyes, the colored part, are blue jade. I do not usually lavish such attention on the eyes." The old man was understandably proud of this piece.

"Blonde-haired, blue-eyed. I'd sure like to meet her," Derek half joked.

"Oh, no, that isn't possible," said the old man, too quickly.

"Deceased?" The question fell from his lips before

he had a chance to check it, and he instantly regretted his *faux pas*. The old man appeared to take no umbrage though.

"Oh no, she is still with us." *Estranged then,* thought Derek. He felt bad for the old man.

"I'll take it," he said, gently setting the doll on the counter.

"Your niece will love it," the old man beamed.

Doubtless she would have, but someone at Derek's office broke the security gate when they propped it open with a brick, and he had to come in on Sunday – the day of her party – to wait for the repairman. Then he got a flat on the crosstown and it was a full hour before AAA arrived with a spare. By the time he got home, his niece was snug in her bed, visions of whatever newly-minted nine-year-olds concerned themselves with dancing in her head.

The doll stared at him from its transitory home on the mantel above his fireplace.

"Sorry, doll," he said, smirking at the wordplay. "I'll take you to your forever home next weekend." He could have simply mailed the doll, he supposed, but that seemed so impersonal. Besides, he hated the idea that it might be damaged in transit.

It was so delicate. So pretty.

He'd been staring at it for several minutes before he snapped out of reverie.

He tossed and turned that night, his dreams fretful things, of beauty and loss and a great wrong that only he could right. He couldn't remember the details in the morning, but they would haunt him throughout the day, nonetheless.

"Morning, doll," he said to the doll as he entered the living room, less amused by his own banter the second time around. "I should give you a name," he decided. Of course, it was probably his niece's job to name her toy. Well, she could always change it later. What did the old man say his daughter's name was? The one who'd provided the doll's likeness? Rachel? Rebecca? Something R. He frowned. It seemed inordinately important that he remember.

"Rebecca, that was it."

He stared at the doll.

It was so lifelike. Almost absurdly beautiful. He wondered again at the girl who had inspired it. How long ago? Judging from the doll's appearance, she wasn't much older than twenty when she sat for it. But how long ago was that? A year? A decade? Maybe the old man worked off a photograph, and she was in her dotage now.

Yet, somehow, he knew she wasn't.

"You're amazing," he said, and gave the doll a kiss on the top of its head.

The hair, *her* hair, smelled ever so slightly of jasmine.

He kept the doll. His niece received a $100 gift card in the mail.

He dreamt of Rebecca every night now, dreams he remembered. Golden tresses resting lightly on bare, pale shoulders; lips full and dark like ripe, black cherries; translucent nightdress, simultaneously clinging and flowing, as could only occur in a certain kind of dream. She called to him; her friend, her lover, her knight-errant. She *needed* him.

Many would have seen in this the long shadow of the uncanny. Signs and portents. *The Twilight Zone.* But not Derek. He knew better. Because he had been through this before.

Obsessions, fixations.

Nikki; dark-haired, mildly exotic. In fifth grade she dressed as Wonder Woman for Halloween. He followed her home after tricks and treats, and, too nervous to ring the front bell, peeped in her windows, hoping to catch sight of her. His parents had been called.

Middle school; Erin. A goddess. He dared not approach her, but he called her house, hundreds of times, hanging up whenever anyone answered.

High school; Lisa. This time, the police were involved.

Nadya. Lynn. Jenny. Another Jenny.

Derek was no stranger to romantic compulsions, and while they had not served him well, something told him that this time...

This time.

He returned to the doll maker's shop.

Initially cunning, ultimately demanding, he found out what he wanted.

Not deceased. Not estranged. The old man lived in rooms above the shop, and she lived with him.

No, he couldn't meet her.

No, he couldn't call on her.

He was to leave immediately. Not come back. Or there would be trouble.

Fine.

Fine.

Because Derek Valentine didn't take *no* for an answer.

He staked out the shop, waited. She had to leave sometime.

But she didn't.

The old man left occasionally, always carefully

securing the store. But Derek never saw the girl. Didn't she have any friends? Any outside responsibilities? Was she bedridden? Or was it something else?

The old man often brought back food for two when he returned from his little sojourns, so Derek knew someone else was there. Someone no one ever saw. And he began to worry this, to pick at it.

Was Rebecca the old man's prisoner?

Why else be so defensive, so secretive? Certainly, an adult woman was capable of rejecting an unwanted suitor without her elderly father's assistance. Something was amiss, and Derek was going to get to the bottom of it.

The old man worked late, and nearly every night, around 1 A.M., he ducked around the corner to the all-night market and bought himself a little treat. A candy bar, a doughnut, a fancy cup of sugar with a little coffee in it. The entire adventure generally took him just under twelve minutes. Derek had timed it.

One night, finally, inevitably, he neglected to lock the shop.

Derek slipped out of his car, approached the door, looked furtively up and down the night-deserted street, then stepped inside. All the lights were on, papers spread on the counter. The old man was doing paperwork. At the far end of the store, obvious now that he was looking for it, a door that undoubtedly opened to the stairs leading to the rooms above.

"What's this now?!"

Behind him. The old man had returned for some forgotten item. A beat, and then he lunged – as much as a frail old man can lunge – for the antiquated telephone resting on the counter. But Derek got there first, wrenching it from the old man's grasp and hurling it aside. It dinged once, pathetically, as it struck the wall.

"Get out! Get out!" the old man shouted. He didn't recognize Derek, merely thought him some random intruder. His hands dropped behind the counter and came up with a heavy wooden stick, a gnarled cane of some sort, and he swung this wildly, connecting with Derek's skull.

Derek saw stars.

Furious, he rushed the old man, relieved him of his stick. It was a shillelagh, he dimly recalled, an Irish walking stick that could double as a bludgeon, although why his brain decided that this was important right now would forever remain a mystery. Raising the shillelagh over his head, he brought it down. Once. Twice. After six times he lost count.

The old man was dead.

What have I done? Panic set in, threatened to engulf him, but he quickly regained his composure. He would simply leave, immediately. They would blame a burglar.

But...

But what if the girl *were* being held against her will?

Perhaps the old man had been hurting her, abusing her. Perhaps he wasn't even her father. Or, worse, perhaps he was. Maybe he, Derek, had saved her. Maybe he was a hero.

He held onto this as he slowly climbed the stairs. If he was wrong, he could still flee, into the night. The girl couldn't identify him. They would blame a burglar.

A short hallway culminating in a kitchenette. Two

doors. The nearest was off the latch. It opened slowly, creaking on rusty hinges. Dark, but a woman's bedroom, clearly a woman's bedroom.

His eyes adjusted and he inhaled sharply. She stood before him, next to the bed, as if she had just climbed out of it. Porcelain skin, flowing locks, azure eyes wide and unblinking. The old man hadn't lied. She *was* a dead ringer for the doll, in every aspect. Because she was, quite literally, a gigantic puppet. Wooden hands reached for him. He couldn't even find a scream.

(Un)Screwed

"The longest screw" sounds like it would be a pretty good time, but it wasn't. Allow me to explain.

The longest screw was an actual, literal screw, discovered approximately eighty kilometers west of Adrar, Algeria after an epic, record-breaking sandstorm which lasted for nine days. At first, nobody was sure *what* it was, this flat, circular metal cap, exactly 600 meters wide, bisected by a single groove, twelve inches deep. Initially it was taken to be the roof of an extensive subterranean weapons cache, or maybe a hidden missile silo, although what a missile silo would be doing way out here, buried under the Saharan dunes, did present something of a mystery. It was quickly determined, however, that this metal disc was set in a much larger expanse of metal, extending for about a kilometer in every direction, and it was further determined that while the disc was flush with this larger sheet of metal, it was clearly a separate piece and could therefore, theoretically, be removed. At this point, of course, everyone still assumed that it was some sort of door. It was only after chipping away at the highly-resistant alloy it was set in for several days that we discovered it was the head of a gigantic, threaded screw.

Now the focus shifted on getting the screw out. Several methods were proposed, none in any way practical. One poor nitwit suggested slotting a large, flat piece of steel into the groove, dangling this from a helicopter, and then spinning the helicopter around and around in circles until the screw was extracted. I pity the poor pilot tasked with *that* assignment. Someone else suggested a similar scheme, but using two rockets. As it turned out, a long, metal pole, engineered to fit into the groove, coupled with simple manpower (consisting of volunteers trucked in from Adrar) was enough to get the extraction started. After several dozen full turns though the enormous screw extended a good five feet out of the ground with no end in sight, so we were forced to build a scaffolding to continue. We added onto the scaffolding when the extracted portion of the screw reached a height of ten feet, and again at sixteen feet, when our jury-rigged scaffolding became too rickety and unwieldy for the workers to continue and was abandoned. At this point we had no choice; we had to bring some real engineers in.

The engineers were amused that we were having so much trouble with a simple screw, until they saw it. They pondered and debated and measured and pondered some more, and finally decided that they would need more money to solve the problem than we had access to. Ultimately, they insisted we inform the proper authorities, if for no other reason than that the proper authorities, when suitably motivated, have access to limitless amounts of money. So we did, and after months of governmental red tape a plan was finally approved to build a gigantic extractor that could be slotted into the screw and, when activated, would climb a full six stories on four grooved, spiral mounts while slowly rotating in a counter-clockwise direction, effectively extracting the screw. It worked beautifully, until it reached its maximum height and the screw still hadn't been entirely extracted.

Another round of red tape, and the extractor was extended, to a full ten stories this time. Finally, when the head of the screw loomed over 30 meters above our heads, there was an audible **POP** and it canted to one side. Cheers erupted all around, until we felt the ground shift beneath our feet and an immense portion of desert rapidly rose into the air, a wall of smooth, flat steel bursting out of the ground in front of us to a height of nearly 150 meters. Once released by the removal of the screw, what turned out to be a gigantic metal plate had rotated on a pair of enormous spring hinges, raising one end of an extensive portion of the desert into the air, an immense ramp jutting out of the desert sands at (approximately) a 30° angle. It was a door, after all. An gargantuan panel, held in place with that single, gigantic screw. Now it had been unlatched, but would we be able to open it completely?

Fully opening the panel, it turned out, was much easier than removing the screw. Grappling the edge at the top of the raised end, two heavy-lift helicopters, working in unison, were ultimately able to raise it to its full height and past the 90° point (in relation to the ground), at which they released it and sent it crashing down into the desert, whipping up so much sand that the area was unapproachable for the better part of a day. When the dust finally, literally settled, all of us – scientist, engineer, and day laborer alike – approached the massive portal as one. But if anyone among us expected to discover an incalculable cache of treasure within, or the remnants of a long-forgotten civilization, they were sorely disappointed.

It was empty. Just a huge, cavernous, empty space, the walls smooth and featureless, the floor consisting of two long, smooth, concave surfaces, bisected by a raised ridge in the middle. On opposite ends of these concavities, mounted into the walls, were two massive, copper coils. That was all. The only other thing of note was discovered later, on the inner surface of the gargantuan panel. A series or runes, language unknown. It took a fair amount of time, but linguists managed to decipher and read these, eventually:

Earth (Terra)
To function properly, requires
two (2) ZZ batteries (not included)

The First Ghetto Hen Born, Booming, as an Institution

On television, they discuss the woman who has killed all of her lovers. They call her the "Praying Mantis" because a praying mantis eats its consort after the act, even though she didn't actually eat her lovers. At least the people on television never say that she did, and that is something they would mention on television. I think they should call her the "Black Widow", but perhaps that name is already taken.

"I want to have sex with that woman," I tell Juan. "Why?" he asks, "So that she can kill you?" "No," I respond, "Just to say I did it. I'll have been the only one. The only living man to have been with the 'Praying Mantis'. I'll be in magazines and tell the story at parties. People will ask me to speak at the Rotary Club. Women will desire me." "Aren't you afraid she'll kill you?" he asks. "She's in custody now," I say, "I'm sure whoever is in charge won't allow THAT to happen." Juan agrees that they probably wouldn't.

We drive to the place where they took her, an asylum in upstate New York. It is named after a doctor long dead, and painted a disheartening shade of peach. The head of the institution meets with us right away, he has no other appointments. "I want to have sex with the 'Praying Mantis'," I tell him. "Her name is Melanie," he corrects me. "You may have sex with her if she consents," he continues, "but you must do it in the day room, in front of myself and the other patients. It will be invaluable to my research." "Did she eat her victims?" asks Juan. "No," says the Doctor, "She stabbed them, with a French cook knife." "You don't let her have a French cook knife NOW?" I ask. "Oh, no," he laughs, "only a butter knife." "I don't even want her to have a butter knife," I insist. He agrees to temporarily take her butter knife. I sign some papers and we go to the day room.

In the day room, Melanie sits watching talk shows on television. The other patients ignore us, except for a bald man who keeps pointing at me and laughing. "Melanie," says the Doctor, "this is __________. Would you be willing to have sex with him?" She looks me over. "Okay." We do it and the Doctor takes notes. She is not particularly attractive or enthusiastic in her lovemaking, but I am the only one. Afterward the Doctor says "That was very useful for my research. Perhaps I will take out an ad in the paper." "No, no!" I insist, "I want to be the only one." "It will make such a good story at parties," agrees Juan. "But my research..." presses the Doctor. "_____ your research," I say. "I shall make her my Bride."

The Priest holds the ceremony in the day room. The Doctor is irritated and refuses to attend. Juan is my Best Man. "...do you take this woman..." I am pensive. "...to have and to hold..." I wish she HAD stabbed me, stabbed me with her butter knife. Most of the patients ignore us, but the bald man continues to point, and laugh.

Emma-Sue Is a Cheap Fuck

The Dark One wore a red baseball cap and expensive sunglasses, like the ones the famous actor wore in that movie last year. He was driving a big, square, American car that belched clouds of blue smoke as it cruised slowly down the street. The car was loud too; backfiring, rattling, with an engine that gave off a maddening staccato that suggested it had thrown a rod. It was this – literally – infernal racket that made the girl on the porch look up, and when she did, she caught His eye. She was white trash, no doubt about it; it was all but tattooed on the small of her back. But she was beautiful, no, scratch that, Scratch corrected, that wasn't the word for it. Not beautiful. Sexy. Arousing. Slim figure; long, reddish-brown hair that fell all too easily on pale shoulders; a top one size too small emphasizing her breasts; sleek, smooth legs that went up and up, until they were interrupted by short, tight, cut-off jeans. All this, thought the Dark One, for the price of a six pack, or a joint, or maybe just a lie: *"Of course I love you."* But, despite His reputation, the Dark One did not lie. He didn't have to.

The girl stared as the Dark One brought His loud, square, American car to an idle, blue exhaust swirling around Him like a poisonous fog. She knew who He was, what He was, and a chill skipped down her nerve endings like a pebble across a pond. But she only hesitated for a moment before she stood, slowly descended the stairs, and approached the car with a practiced confidence she didn't quite feel. She instinctively stopped just out of arm's reach, opened her mouth, and realized that she had nothing to say.

"Do you party?" asked the Dark One sarcastically, both because it was such a delightful cliché and because He already knew the answer. The girl hesitated for a moment, then, without a word, walked around the front of the vehicle. She flinched as he revved the engine, but didn't break her stride. Sliding into the passenger seat, she saw two of her neighbors watching with disgust. But was it aimed at her, or Him? Both? The square American car pulled away, backfiring loudly. Both neighbors jumped at the sound, and this made her smile, but only for a moment. The Dark One laughed, but He wasn't looking at the startled busybodies, so she wasn't sure if He was laughing because of them, or something else.

Neither of them spoke. The Dark One cruised along at well under the speed limit, smiling a toothy smile like a white picket fence and occasionally lifting His hand in a slow half-wave when people took notice of them. Most of these people quickly looked away, and a few even dropped what they were doing and immediately scampered inside. This made the girl feel sad, and strangely guilty, as if it were somehow her fault.

Finally, the Dark One brought his loud, ugly car to a halt in front of a nondescript house. They were still in the neighborhood, but she knew that she would never be able to find this house again, no matter how long she looked. The engine cut off automatically, with no prompting from Him. He got out and, without a word, made for the front door. The girl knew that He expected her to follow, so she did, unconsciously rubbing the crotch of her shorts as she trailed Him across the dead lawn, into the dark house, and upstairs.

"Lie down," He commanded, and she did. The Dark One removed His hat and His expensive, popular sunglasses, and while she'd half expected His eyes to be empty and black, or possibly red, dancing with the fires of Hell, they were, in fact, blue, a blue so clear and deep that they reminded her of the way the ocean looks in dreams, or rose-colored memories. "Truth be told, I was in the mood for a little boy today," He said, "but for some reason you caught my eye." She flushed. "What's your name?" He asked, which was absurd because she knew that He already knew the answer.

"Emma-Sue," she told Him anyway. He paused.

"What a stupid name," He mumbled. "Stupid name for a stupid, stupid girl." She almost cried. "How old are you, Emma?" He asked, with mock indifference.

"Twenty," she managed, hurt by His words.

"Ah."

"What's *your* name?" she whispered, because she needed to say something.

"You know who I am." He pulled off her shorts and she waited for the inevitable pain of his thrust, but it was gentle, and *good,* oh so good. He sped up and she could feel, actually feel, her soul being drawn out of her body.

The Dark One stared at Emma-Sue's lifeless husk as He tightened his belt. He'd felt giddy, almost high, as long as the effect had lasted, but her soul had been far from pure, and He was already hungry again.

"Cheap fuck," He muttered.

Limbs

One spring, the limbs on all the trees
Sprouted hands instead of leaves.
The children were overjoyed
As this made climbing the old oak
All the easier,
And the handsome shade
Under the sycamore that summer
Was particularly conductive
To sipping lemonade.
All was well until autumn came,
When the falling hands
Created a cacophony of applause
That drowned out all other sounds.
Arrogantly, the squirrels took a bow.

Hallucitopia

1

The storm had washed something up from the bay, Mitch noticed as he stepped onto the back patio. It looked like a chrome party balloon, but an unusual one, to say the least. Black as night, speckled with larger and smaller flecks of color – red, yellow, blue, green. As he meandered down to the waterline to examine it, sipping his reheated coffee, he realized that it was far too weighty to be a balloon. He stared, mildly dumbfounded. Knelt down, tapped it with a curious fingernail.

It was a *rock*. Irregular, about the size of an elongated football, the flecks of color were actually mica-like veins and deposits embedded in the larger whole, which was smooth and non-reflective and dark as a miner's asshole. It was heavy, too. Dense. He toed it and had a hard time rolling it over, although the fact that it was comfortably settled in the sucking mud didn't help any. No way this *washed up* from anywhere; it would've sunk right to the bottom. And it certainly hadn't been unearthed by the tide. The ground it sat in hadn't eroded that much in one night. So where had it come from? Whatever the case, it was quite pretty, and certainly unusual, so, gripping it with both hands, he pulled it free and lugged it up the yard and onto the deck. He forgot all about the cup of coffee. Placing the rock carefully on one of his heavy wooden deck chairs, he located the hose, dragged it

83

over, realized he needed to turn it on, went back, twisted the spigot, and raced the water back, beating it by a couple of seconds. He held the hose loosely over his prize, letting the water dribble languidly out, taking his time. Rinsed clean of mud and sand and salt water its blackness only intensified until it seemed to eat the light, the colorful impurities(?) standing out in stark, glittering contrast. He wracked his brain, tried to dredge up some high school geology. The thing it most resembled, he decided, was glass. A huge, honking chunk of glass, worn smooth by the ocean. But it didn't *feel* like glass. He stroked the surface again—

—and found himself flat on his ass, fogged vision clearing, his right hand in something wet and sticky. He held it up. Blood. But not his, a puddle of it, pooling up next to him, spilling out of a long organic tube of disembodied intestine laying next to him on the ground...

He scream-gagged and, instantly, everything was normal again. Well, mostly. He *had* fallen on his ass, and his right hand *was* wet, from the puddle of water forming next to him where he'd dropped the hose. But he could *smell* the blood, the copper, organic-ness of it. Then this, too, faded.

What. The. Fuck?

A stroke. It must have been. Shaken, shaking, he located his keys and his insurance card and drove to the emergency room.

2

It hadn't been a stroke. It hadn't been anything, actually, that they could find, though it was,

84

admittedly, a cursory examination. "Stress," the physician on call suggested. "But I'm going to recommend a CAT scan." Stress. What did he have to be stressed about? He made the appointment, drove six blocks out of the way for a replacement coffee – a good one, this time, from Starbucks – and went back home to his empty, waterfront house.

And his rock.

He had almost forgotten about the rock. It was still on the deck, blithely absorbing the late afternoon sunlight like a hole in space, the colored flecks suspended within, twinkling. Like stars. He felt a sudden pang, seeing it out there. Someone could have stolen it. Just wandered into his back yard and walked off with it. He wondered, vaguely, if it were worth anything. Maybe it was a meteorite. That actually made a lot of sense. Just dropped down out of the sky while he'd slumbered. Or maybe it fell out of an airplane. Regardless, he'd have to bring it inside.

He hesitated. Went to the shed and found some gardening gloves first. Why am I afraid to touch it, he wondered?

You know why.

He got it inside, swept aside some work and placed it on the dining room table, which doubled as his desk. His nose tingled. There was the merest hint of a scent emanating from it, sort of coconut-banana. But artificial, like something that was supposed to smell or taste "tropical". He sat down, removed his gloves, set them aside, and then stared at the rock. He felt a strong, silly urge to name it. "Harold" or something. Better yet, "Dwayne". He smiled.

He decided to touch it again. Deliberately, this

time. But first he cleared his mind, doused his anxieties. Happy thoughts. Happy thoughts.

He pressed his palm against its smooth surface.

For several seconds nothing happened, and then the colorful impurities began to sparkle. Within moments his hand began to tingle, and this sensation traveled up his arm until his entire body was pleasantly numb, like he'd inhaled a hefty dose of nitrous oxide.

With detached interest, he noticed something creeping across the table, undulating like an inchworm. It was a pencil! Amazing. He watched it for several seconds, until it reached the edge of the table and fell off. No doubt about it, he was hallucinating. He removed his hand from the rock and reality hit him like a slap in the face, so jarring he had to catch his breath.

Mother of fuck. He'd better call somebody. But who?

3

"So why call me?" Devden asked. "Not that I'm complaining."

"Well, you were pre-med for a while, so I figured you might have some insight. You know, as to the medical... physicality, whatever."

"My endless cross to bear. Not only does everyone in my extended family think I'm good for free medical advice, but I'm a perpetual disappointment to my parents for not going through with it." Devden shook his head.

"My guess is that it's giving off some sort of gas or something," Mitch said.

"So you brought it into your house? Brilliant."
Devden crouched down and looked closely at it. "I
don't smell anything. It's so *black*. Like Vantablack."

"What's Vantablack?"

"It's a light-absorbing artificial material. Google
it," Devden said.

"Do you think that's what this is?" Mitch asked.

"I doubt it. I mean, it's pretty damned unlikely.
Where did you get it?"

"I found it on the ground," Mitch said with the hint
of a grin.

"Ha ha."

"No, really, I found it out back, down by the water.
At first I thought the storm washed it up, until I
realized how heavy it was. Now I'm thinking meteor,
maybe?"

"Hmm," Devden said noncommittally.

"Touch it," Mitch suggested.

"I don't think I ought to. There might be some sort
of contact poison coating it. That's what could be
giving you your little 'trips'." He stood up. "Listen, I
know a guy over at the university who used to work
for the Madiport institute."

"Used to?"

"He got canned for diddling a student. Kind of a
creep, but stupid smart. I'd like to take him a piece of
this thing, if I could."

Mitch shrugged.

"Sure."

"Got a hammer and chisel?"

"In the shed. Let me carry it outside first so you
don't demolish my dinner table."

He wore the gloves. The tools were where he
always kept them. He was organized.

"Safety goggles?" Devden asked. Mitch shook his head.

"I could scrounge up a pair of wraparound sunglasses."

"It'll have to do."

Devden placed the chisel against the rock and raised the hammer. Mitch cringed. He wasn't sure what he was afraid would happen – an explosion; the rock emitting a human-like scream – but nothing unusual occurred and a fist-sized piece broke off at the first blow. It was a relatively smooth break, like shale, and now they could see that the colorful "impurities" permeated the entire object. The newly revealed face was deep grey rather than black, but within the hour it would steadily darken until it blended perfectly with the rest of the exposed surface.

"Get me a Tupperware container," Devden said.

"How about a baggie?" Mitch suggested. He didn't want to part with his good Tupperware.

"This isn't an ounce of skunk weed. Tupperware."

It took Mitch several minutes to find one with a matching lid. Devden scooted his sample inside and sealed it up.

"Okay, I'll get this over to Gary..." he checked his watch. It was getting late. The sun, just about to kiss the horizon, confirmed this. "First thing tomorrow. In the meantime, I wouldn't touch it. Like I said, it could be a contact poison. Or maybe something that lives in a hole in it popped out and stung you."

"I've already been to the ER," Mitch said. "Clean."

"And they tested you for every possible contingency during this sole visit to the ER?"

Mitch frowned. He hadn't considered that.

"Exactly. I'll get this to Gary. We'll call you."

Consequences be damned, Mitch couldn't wait for Devden to leave, so he could touch it again.

But first, a witness.

Better yet, a partner in crime.

He called Lina.

"Hey, double L," he said to her voice mail. Her last name was LaCoste. "Call back. Call back call back callback callback callbackcallbackcallback." He ended the call. Two seconds later she called back.

"What are you doing, right now?" he asked before she said a word.

"Right this second? Folding my t-shirts into little squares. It's laundry day."

"Wanna get high?"

"Maybe?"

"Wanna get high in a way you've never gotten high before?"

"Not sure. Could you expound on that?"

He expounded.

"If I come all the way over there, and this is some kind of a joke, you owe me dinner."

"Deal."

When she got there, the rock was back inside, on the table. She was wearing loose sweatpants and a men's t-shirt, her standard "getting dangerously high" attire. "Dress for comfort, that's my motto," she always said. She also brought a half gallon of orange juice, and a box of sugar cubes.

"You want to keep you blood sugar up when you're using hallucinogens," she explained. "Prevents bad trips."

"Where'd you get that?"

"From Joey's book." Joseph Mellen. She always referred to famous people in familiar terms, as if she knew them personally.

"The 'drill a hole in your head to get permanently high' guy?"

"'That would've worked if you hadn't stopped me.'" Quoting *Ghostbusters*. She crouched down, got eye-level with the rock. "So this is it? It's so *black*."

"Right? If it wasn't for the colored flecks it would look like a hole in the air."

She reached out to touch it, hesitated, pulled up a chair so that she was seated comfortably, and then cracked open her orange juice, added several sugar cubes, and drank about a quarter of it down. Then she closed her eyes and placed her hand on the rock.

She inhaled suddenly, almost but not quite a gasp. She smiled, her eyes still closed.

"Wow," she said.

"What?"

"Colors, behind my eyelids. Like the flakes in the rock. But more colors, the whole spectrum." Her brow crinkled. "I don't know that one..." she said to herself, with a touch of confusion.

"Try opening your eyes," Mitch said.

"I'm almost afraid to. This is so intense, so immediate." She did though, and looked around the room in awe.

"What do you see?"

"Fucking *colors*, Mitch. You don't know the half of it! Holy fucking shit, I never knew there were so *many*. There's, like, entirely new *spectrums*..." She turned to him. Her smile was so wide it must have hurt. "How long does this last?"

"Just a few seconds, as far as I can tell."

She frowned.

"Yeah, it's fading already." She perched on the chair, Native American style, and studied the rock. "Where did you *get* this?"

"I found it."

"Really?"

"Really."

"Does anyone else know about it?"

"Devden."

"Ugh, that tightass? You called him before you called me?"

"He's smart."

"Counter argument: I have bigger tits."

"That's why you're here now, and he isn't," Mitch grinned.

They shared a mischievous look.

"It is Friday..." Lina began.

"Is it?"

"That gives us two whole days, and then some. Wanna get freaky?"

"How freaky?"

"*Real* freaky. Like covered in cooking oil, rolling around together with this thing in the shower freaky."

He was already starting to undress.

5

Devden made it to the college late the next morning and turned the sample over to Gary Mitre (*Dr. Mitre* to his associates), with plans to follow up in a couple of days. But then life happened. A semi-panicky phone call at 11 PM. His father was short of breath, his left arm tingling. Devden's stepmother had rushed him to the ER. A heart attack, a mild one. He'd have to make some lifestyle changes, but was in no immediate danger. Two days observation, max. But Devden felt he should be there, so he caught the first plane to Philly and hovered bedside and comforted his stepmother and reluctantly participated in the inevitable arguments about whether or not Dad was *finally* going to quit smoking (he was, insisted his wife), and what sort of exercise regimen he was going to take up (none, insisted Dad), and by the time the dust cleared and the compromises had been made (minimal exercise, no more smoking) and Devden got back home and caught up on the work he'd neglected three weeks had somehow passed him by.

Only then did he remember the sample.

He drove to campus as soon as he could get away.

"Dev!" Gary beamed. "Jesus Christ am I glad to see you!" He gripped Devden's shoulder with his free hand as they shook. "I tried to call, but it turns out I have an old number...?"

"Cripes, I'm sorry. Some stuff came up, my dad's had some health issues..."

"Think nothing of it. You have to tell me, though – where did you find that mineral sample?"

"On the beach." Close enough to the truth.

"Well, come with me. You're not going to believe this." He led Devden down first one hallway, then another, deep into the building. Finally, they reached a heavy steel door. Gary punched a seven digit code into the alphanumeric keypad on the wall next to it. 3-8-2-5-9-6-8. Devden suspected that Gary's pass code was probably *fuckyou.*

"I'm doing some government work, off the books," Gary explained. "So anything you see not pertaining to your sample, just pretend you didn't, okay?"

The door swung open. A beady-eyed man in a lab coat turned away from the centrifuge he was monitoring and glared at them. "Who the hell is this?" the man asked.

"Zip it, Ross. He's with me."

Ross zipped it, but he didn't look happy about it.

"Don't look," Gary said, covering Devden's eyes with one hand. "La la la la la, top secret, nothing to see here." They walked a fair distance and then stepped through a door which Gary closed behind them before removing his hand.

They were in a medium-sized, white room. On a sizable steel table before them a convoluted maze had been constructed with interlocking pieces of corrugated plastic sheets. At the center of the maze sat the sample. Surrounding the sample, dozens of dead mice, and several living specimens, the latter rubbing themselves against it maniacally, like over-affectionate house cats doped up on catnip.

"What *is* this?" Devden asked.

"This," Gary said, "is Stage 3."

"Stage 3?"

"Ask me about Stages 1 and 2." He was grinning from ear to ear.

"Okay, Gary. Tell me about Stages 1 and 2."

"Your sample, whatever it is – it's a mineral; I mean, I've determined that much – is addictive. But it's not *physically* addictive, or even psychologically addictive. It's more... Okay, for lack of a better word, *socially* addictive."

"I don't get you."

"Okay. So you warned me about the alleged hallucinogenic properties, but I didn't have time to run a whole battery of tests, so the first thing I did was pick it up with a pair of tongs and drop it into a vivarium full of your friend and mine, *Periplaneta americana*, AKA the giant, Florida cockroach. Just looking for a basic reaction, sub-lizard brain stuff. I primarily wanted to see if they'd approach it or avoid it or ignore it or what. Well I got a reaction, all right – they went berserk. Swarming all over it, thrashing around for a while like they'd been poisoned, then taking flight and just flying in circles, colliding with each other – they can fly, you know, but they almost never do because they can run so much faster – and finally attacking each other and fighting to the death. It was a cockroach bloodbath."

"Death metal band name alert," Devden said.

"Right? You should write that one down. Anyway, there was a really interesting paper by these three jokers – Lihoreau, Costa, and R-something – about social dynamics as observed in traditionally non-social insects, and how these 'non-social' insects do in fact have their own social structures and often behave cooperatively. Well, it's as if extended contact with your sample broke that down entirely, triggered a sort of 'every roach for himself' mentality. They went on a sociopathic rampage. But I suspect that was just a case of crossed wires, I think because they couldn't process what exposure to the sample was trying to impart to them."

"I'm totally lost here."

"Okay, we'll move on. My next experiment was with the mice. Highly social, and with considerably higher cognitive abilities, of course. Put the sample at the center of the maze and placed them at various points, with food and water stockpiled in strategic locations, forcing them to explore. When they located the sample they went koo-koo bananas for it too. Remember that experiment where they gave rats cocaine and after a while the rats would stop depressing the lever that delivered food and just kept triggering the one that delivered more cocaine? I thought I had a similar thing going, but when I finally tore myself away from my other responsibilities long enough to really observe them for an unbroken period of time I realized that a very crazy thing was happening. They were fucking obsessed with the sample, with being in contact with it, but they were obsessing over it in *shifts*. Individuals were actually tagging out, for want of a better term, so that they could navigate the maze back to the point where the food and water was without leaving the sample unattended. Unattended, hell. *Unutilized*."

"That's really strange."

"Oh, I haven't even gotten to the best part. The recruits."

"Recruits?"

"Yeah. 'Converted' mice – ones who had become addicted to contact with the stone – would 'tag out' and then go through one-way doors into other parts of the maze and try to lead unaffected mice back with them, like little mice zealots. They lost their minds when they couldn't get back through the one-way doors. Threw themselves against the walls, tried to climb over, chew their way through. Some of them went totally berserk and took it out on their potential initiates, turning on them and tearing them to pieces. When I swapped out the one-way doors for two-ways and introduced a new generation to the maze, the converts immediately tracked them down and 'converted' them, too. They also dragged all the dead mice into the space with the sample, although I don't know what *that's* about. Maybe the converts are so wonked out they don't realize that their buddies are dead."

Devden was trying to process all this.

"It's fucking dangerous," he finally said. "I mean, right? This thing could fuck a *person* up just as easily..." Shit. Mitch.

"Well," Gary said. "That's assuming a lot. With higher cognitive ability comes..."

Devden wasn't listening. He was already out the door.

6

They grabbed him the instant he burst out of the misappropriated room. Guards, but not campus security. Weird uniforms that he didn't recognize. *What are you doing here? Let's see some identification! Do you know how much trouble you're in?* Vague threats were thrown around, words like *terrorist* and *felony*. Gary treated it like a joke, rolling his eyes and repeatedly cracking wise. Like he was a movie theater usher who'd snuck a friend into the show. Two men in suits, radiating importance, showed up in short order and confronted everybody. When one of these men coolly "reminded" Gary that this laboratory wasn't his own, private playground he told the man to go fuck himself. It was a parade of clusterfuck that took over an hour to sort out. Fucking Gary.

It was late afternoon by the time Devden reached his car, and as he sped towards Mitch's house he was pretty sure that a big black sedan was following him, for a while.

But that wasn't important. What was important was that he get that freaky goddamned rock away from Mitch.

Mitch's neighborhood was strangely quiet. No kids playing, no one jogging or walking their dog. Houses shut up tight, blinds drawn. It wasn't warm enough to be shutting out the sun or cranking the AC. Devden had a funny feeling in the pit of his stomach.

He didn't see anyone until he reached Mitch's place. There, on the lawn, nearly a dozen people, men and women, milling about. They stared at him as he pulled into the drive, parked. Something off about them, but he didn't have time to process it. Dismissing them, he let himself in the front door, down the hallway...

The rock was still on the dining room table. Except it had been shattered into a hundred pieces.

Thank you, Lord Vishnu.

Only then did he notice the elephant in the room. Lina, naked, sprawled across the sofa and absently stimulating herself with the handle of a spatula. Well, not entirely naked. She was wearing a choker, boasting a small, irregular stone so black that it looked like she had a bullet hole in her throat.

Oh no.

"Hello, Dev."

Mitch stepped into the room, from the kitchen. He wore blue jeans but no shirt, the piece of stone hanging from his neck resting comfortably against his bare chest.

"Mitch..." Devden began, but then held his tongue. It was no use. Better to slip away, get away, and call the police, or the CDC, or somebody.

"Just checking up on you," Devden said. He tried to sound casual, but his voice broke.

"I'm fine. Great." He indicated Lina. "We're all great." Striding over the the dining room table, he selected a tiny piece of rock. "Got one for you." He held it up, barely a chip.

"I had one for lunch," Devden said, forcing a laugh. It came out as more of a cough.

"Touch it," Mitch said, holding it out.

Devden changed tactics.

"It's dangerous, Mitch."

"It's not dangerous, Dev. It's no more dangerous than walking into another room. Because that's what it is. A *door*. A door to another room that we've been locked out of for *far* too long."

"What's in this... room, Mitch?"

"Glory." He stepped closer, held the chip up to Devden's face. "Touch it. Just for a second."

"That's all?" Devden asked. "Just for a second? And that'll be the end of it?"

"Of course," Mitch said, his tone suggesting that he suspected Devden was, perhaps, in the grip of a mild, unjustified paranoia. He waited a beat, to give the next thing he said more gravitas. "But you won't want it to be. The end of it, I mean."

"I won't?"

"No. Please, take a piece with you. Take several. I made necklaces! Convenient and inconspicuous."

"Okay," Devden said. "I won't wear one of your necklaces, but I'll touch it. Just for a second." *And then I'll run like hell*, he thought. He reached out –

– and suddenly powerful arms gripped him from behind, pinning his own arms against his back. One of the men he'd seen outside. The assailant had slipped inside so quietly, crept up on Devden so stealthily, that Devden hadn't even noticed. He struggled to free himself, to no avail.

"I won't!" Devden shouted. "I won't wear it! I'll throw it away the second I leave!"

Mitch shook his head.

"I know you would," he said. He nodded to another unseen person and suddenly large, powerful hands were wrapped around Devden's face, his jaw, prying it open.

"**Glory!** Glory **glory** glory **glory**...!" Lina moan-shouted. She had stimulated herself to orgasm.

Mitch placed the chip on Devden's tongue. One of the large, powerful hands immediately clamped itself over his nose and mouth. He put up a valiant struggle, but he couldn't breathe and eventually he had no choice. He swallowed.

"*Glorygloryglorygloryglory!*" moaned Lina.

"Welcome to Utopia," Mitch said.

We Are the Real
Children of the Corn

"Corn corn corn! I can't take it anymore!"

John tossed the newspaper aside then leaned back and stared at Tess, waiting for her to respond. When she didn't, he prodded her. "It's the number one cash crop in the country, you know! By a ridiculous margin! We devote nearly a hundred million acres to growing it! That's all Americans eat! Corn corn corn! We don't need any more corn!"

"I can't remember the last time we had corn," she said, without looking up from her coffee.

"Corn on the cob, maybe, or out of a can, but it's *everywhere*. Breakfast cereals, snack chips, soup... corn whiskey... everything sugary is sweetened with corn *syrup*. And animal feed is mostly corn, you know, so if we're not eating the damn corn we're eating something that ate the damned corn! Hell, even the filler in *his* food is corn!" He indicated the dog, which hung its head. From the tone of his voice, the animal assumed that it had done something wrong. "I'm telling you, I can't stand it anymore! What's wrong with beets, or broccoli, or asparagus?"

Tess finally looked up.

"It's not too late to sell," she reminded him. "Everyone else has. All our neighbors, our friends, are gone."

"Not everyone," John grumbled.

"Maybe you should take the day off," Tess suggested, not unkindly.

"Gah, no one ever listens, anyway," John said, pushing away from the table. "I'm going into town."

"At least think about it, dear."

Outside, the conglomerate's corn fields were pushing up against his own acreage, isolated stalks already popping up on his side of the property line, as if staking a claim. He fumed and climbed into his truck.

Corn, all around him as he drove into town, creeping right up to the road, stalks filling the roadside ditches and even invading the shoulder. And it wasn't any better in town, either. Lawns blotted out by battalions of corn, corn struggling into the light through cracks in the sidewalk. Vacant lots, parks, even traffic islands had been compromised. It was dimly visible through the haze-dust windows of abandoned houses, having inexorably pushed its way up through the floorboards. Downtown, the road in front of the courthouse had burst asunder, stalks wildly projecting out every which way, so much corn that he couldn't navigate it, even with his truck, the stalks cracking, ears crunching juicily beneath his tires and then jamming in the wheel well. He backed up, tried a different route, no use.

Finally he turned around and drove back to the house, or as close as he could get, anyway. The corn was so thick across the road now – having thrust itself through the asphalt – that he couldn't drive through it if he tried. Furious, he climbed out and began to walk, winding through the stalks, his anger growing by the minute. It took him three hours to get back. A thirty minute walk, previously.

"Tess!" he shouted. "Where are you?" The back yard had been entirely taken over, the front yard sprouting scattered stalks already up to his knees. The dog crawled out from under the house, cowed and whimpering.

"Tess!" he shouted again. Ears of corn pressed against the windows, from the inside, as if they were watching him. When he opened the door, the front hall was dense with pale green-brown and that oddly dusty husk smell. He had to slip sideways between stalks that had come up through the floor to get to the stairs, angrily kicking the ears off particularly zealous individuals that had climbed halfway to the mid-story landing and beyond.

He found her in the bedroom, the corn already sprouting from her body. Feeding on her.

"Damn it all to hell," he said, more irritated than mournful.

Something moved outside, in the corn. He threw open the window and leaned out.

Men, five of them, their features hidden beneath cowls, their forms lost in the folds of monkish robes, robes of a purple so deep as to almost be black. One of them beckoned to him. He fought his way down the stairs, which were almost impassable now. They were waiting.

"This is private property..." John began. The dog whined, concerned that it would be called on to act.

"We appreciate that this is your land," one of the men said. "That's why we're here. It's all gone too far. Amok. Madness. You can see that. That's why we've come for you."

"Just who are you?" John asked, suspicious.

"The Prophets of the Machine."

Pro*phets*? Did he hear that right?

A hand on his shoulder.

"We need you to join our brotherhood. To help us do what *must* be done."

This came across as neither ominous nor ridiculous. It was simply a statement of fact.

"Okay," John said. Defiant or resigned, he didn't know.

They led and he followed, into the corn.

Ironic, yes, but there was nowhere else to go.

The Book of Bob

¹:¹ There was a man in *the* town of Hicksville, Oregon, whose name *was* Bob, and this man was kind of a jerk – *one who* kicked puppies and stole the sheets and towels from Holiday Inn. ¹:² He was married, but had no sons or daughters, and, in truth, would no longer have had a wife if she hadn't misplaced those photographs of him with those sixteen airline stewardesses. ¹:³ This lack of heirs was likely for the best, because if he did have kids he'd probably sell them to gypsies or, at the very least, make *their* curfew ten P.M. on school nights or something equally ridiculous, as parents are wont to do. ¹:⁴ This man owned his own apartment, a '76 Ford Gremlin, and a dog of unspecified breeding, which he conked on the head every so often, just for fun.

²:¹ Now, it came about, for no apparent reason, that one day Satan came into the *presence* of the Lord. ²:² How's it hangin'? Satan asked provocatively, but God, being the divine type at all, ignored this remark. ²:³ Then Satan said, If thou [**you** -Ed.] art [**are** -Ed.] so powerful, then *why is* your creation Bob now my servant? ²:⁴ And so God said, Is this a bet?

³:¹ The following day Bob came home to find a letter from a famous celebrity in his mailbox. ³:² It was Ed McMahon. ³:³ The letter said, You May Already Be a Winner. ³:⁴ Bob opened it. ³:⁵ He was already a winner.

⁴:¹ Later that same day (a Wednesday, incidentally), a

phone call alerted Bob that his mother, who had been sick for *some time*, had miraculously recovered overnight. ⁴⁼² Bob was very happy (after all, medical bills are very high these days), and promised himself that he'd visit her *just as soon* as he got around to it.

⁵⁼¹ Bob was now a millionaire, and a worry-free one. ⁵⁼² So he quit his job. ⁵⁼³ His wife said, Buy me some *new* clothes. ⁵⁼⁴ He pummeled her with a Mixmaster. ⁵⁼⁵ Bob instead chose to indulge in every excess imaginable; he drank, gambled, snorted cocaine, and caroused with women of questionable character until all hours of the morning. ⁵⁼⁶ Bob's wife said, Why don't you change your ways? Donate some money to my new church fund. ⁵⁼⁷ He *brained* her with the toaster oven.

⁶⁼¹ One day, Bob's neighbors were *loitering* outside the 7-11 when Bob sauntered in to buy some beer. ⁶⁼² One of the neighbors, Elmer, pointed at Bob and said, You better watch it, Bob, you're going to lose that cash the same way you got it! ⁶⁼³ You're just jealous, Bob replied, giving Elmer the finger. ⁶⁼⁴ Bill, a friend of Elmer's, sighed. ⁶⁼⁵ The lazy people and assholes always get all the breaks, *Bill* complained. ⁶⁼⁶ Bob heard him and smiled. ⁶⁼⁷ He bought two six packs of Bud Light and a bag of Cheetos.

⁷⁼¹ After *Bob* left, another neighbor spoke up. ⁷⁼² His name was Zophar, and he hated it because in grade school all the other kids made fun of him, saying, Zophar, so good, and such. ⁷⁼³ Anyway, Zophar said, Hey, boys, maybe ol' Bob did *do* something good along the way, and that's why he *fell into* all that cash and doesn't

have to keep up his mother now. ^{7:4} Zophar said, Maybe he deserves it. ^{7:5} After that, Bill and Elmer didn't talk to Zophar much anymore.

^{8:1} Now, about this time, God had had just about enough of Bob. ^{8:2} So He approached *Bob*, on the street, in the form of an old man who smelled vaguely of Italian salad dressing. ^{8:3} Stop, Bob, it is I, your Lord and savior! said God. ^{8:4} Here, you smelly bum, buy a cup of coffee, Bob answered, and flipped *God* a quarter.

^{9:1} God was pissed. ^{9:2} First, he beat the crap out of Bob (God is a black belt). ^{9:3} Next, using *his laptop*, He slashed Bob's credit rating and transferred all the money in his *accounts* to a cat named Leroy who belonged to an old lady in Ohio who had to use a walker to get around and could only eat Jell-O and applesauce because she didn't have any teeth. ^{9:4} *Lastly*, God put a bag of dog *crap* on Satan's porch and set it on fire, since he (Satan) was the one who started all this trouble in the first place.

^{10:1} So *it seemed* Bob's life was no longer blessed, because his dog got hit by a trolley car and his '76 Gremlin got creamed in *the* parking lot. (*The person* who hit it *did leave* a note. It said, Sorry.) ^{10:2} Then his wife ran away with the plumber. ^{10:3} After she took the *last* of his money. ^{10:4} After this lived Bob only a *fortnight*, for he accidentally plunged from his apartment building's roof while trying to hit a pigeon with a rowboat oar.

Sing Those Beautiful Junkyard Dues

Tommi, God bless her, was fascinated by the dump, so after we'd separated and deposited our recyclables (colored glass, clear glass, aluminum, plastic, paper) we showed our IDs (you had to be a county resident to poke around), and passed through the gate into the yard proper. Here, on the fringes, it was mostly large, curbside items, useless and rotting. The big stuff that the garbageman picks up on special days, by appointment. Rarely anything with any secondary value though. Like metals. These are almost always scavenged immediately. Not true *trash*, more what you'd expect to find in a junkyard. Think *Sanford & Son*. No cars, though – they were stockpiled on the far end, when they ended up here at all. Here it was all gutted appliances and beyond useless furniture and the entire spectrum of human jetsam. Headless baby doll, crusty with something foul and organic. Cracked planter in the shape of a watchful rabbit, not cute and anthropomorphized, but realistic and eerily Celtic, it's eyes wild and accusatory. Broken crates and water damaged office goods and irregular lumber and anything and everything. Found an entire set of encyclopedias here, once. Brand new. But who needs encyclopedias, now? The first time I came with Tommi she literally stumbled over a moving box full of compact discs, all hard rock, decent stuff. Like new. Kept what we wanted and sold the rest to what must be the last record/CD store on Earth for a quarter apiece. Walked away with forty bucks, which we split between us and then treated each other to dinner, chain restaurant style.

You weren't supposed to climb the unpredictable piles of junk, so of course we did, cresting the first, carefully working out way down the other side, and then conquering the second. Three more, further than most people ever ventured, and you reached a fence, topped with razor wire. Beyond that, the *real* trash. Household trash: post-consumer paper goods and old food and used diapers. People are such filthy creatures. Filthier, even, than our own off-cast junk. We reached the fence and Tommi clung to it, fingers wrapped around the chain-link, looking in.

"It's still there," she said.

It was. Life-size, fully realized. Likely you could climb inside. Again, I wondered what it was doing here. Probably the studio had just dumped all the props here after the show was canceled, but why had this piece ended up on the other side of the fence, with the used tissues and take-out containers and cat box detritus?

Because someone wanted it, probably, and didn't want people like us to get it.

Tommi rattled the fence. "There has to be a way in."

"There is," I said. "I've walked the perimeter. But it's padlocked."

"So what's the plan?"

"This is purely a reconnaissance mission. We'll see if it can be disassembled, and what we'll need to do that. Likely it's just wood and paint. If the pieces are just screwed together we can come back and disassemble it and toss the pieces over the fence."

"If not?"

"We'll cross that galaxy when we come to it."

"Okay. Boost me up?" Tommi asked, placing her hand on his shoulder in anticipation.

"That's razor wire," I pointed out.

"I think I can navigate it."

"You can't. And anyway, why risk it? We'll wait until dark, break the lock, and replace it with this." I pulled a combination padlock out of my pocket.

"The combination will be wrong," she pointed out.

"So? It's the same brand. They'll just think something's wrong with it and get a new one. Even if they suspect something, they're not going to call in a CSI team because somebody broke into the dump."

"Then why replace the lock at all?"

"Better they not know we were here, if possible. Whoever hid the thing might move it."

"You thought of everything. My genius." She leaned in to kiss me but the wind shifted just then, killing the moment.

Dusk came, summer-late, at which point we made our way along the fence, walking for what felt like forever, our goal out of sight entirely by the time we reached the locked gate. I crouched down, surveyed the scene. The dump closed at five, and it was now almost eight. It seemed safe to proceed. I slipped the absurdly long screwdriver I'd purchased at a close-out store (for a dollar), slid it through the cheap lock, and twisted. The lock held, but the eye it was looped through broke. Ah, well.

"Houdini," Tommi giggled.

We slipped inside.

It was full dark now, but there was a full moon, and we had flashlights. We followed the fence back, on the opposite side this time. Five minutes, ten, thirty. I checked my watch. We must have gone too far.

"Damn it."

"What?"

"I think we passed it."

I made to climb a heap of something, to get a better view, but my foot sunk in to the knee, accompanied by a rancid stench.

"Ugh," I gagged.

"You're not staying over tonight," Tommi joked.

"Hey!" someone shouted. Not one of us.

"Lights!" I hissed and we doused them.

Voices, on the other side of the fence.

"We're not doing anything wrong," Tommi said. The logic of a beautiful young woman who routinely got out of trouble just by batting her eyes.

"We're trespassing," I reminded her. Grabbing her wrist, I pulled her deeper into the yard, away from the fence. A beam of light swung past, missing us as we ducked down. We kept going, at a crouch, until we were sure we were beyond the reach of the beam. I didn't think they saw us. Certainly no one called out, although I thought I heard a voice say something like "Damn kids."

We waited, hesitant to use our own lights. I decided that we should stay put for an hour, just to be safe. By then, even the most committed security guard would say to hell with it, especially since he was literally just guarding trash. When I finally did trigger my light, only the palest glow emerged. "Damn it," I said.

"What?"

"My light's dead." I dramatically tossed it over my shoulder in an ironic gesture, hoping she picked up on my wit. "We'll have to rely on yours."

"I've been turning mine on and off for the last five minutes. Nada."

Shit.

It took me several minutes to locate the flashlight I'd so casually tossed aside, and by the time I found it, I was completely rank.

"Jesus Christ," Tommi said, holding her nose. "If you were in my toilet I wouldn't even bother to flush. I'd just burn the whole house down."

"Screw you," I said. My sense of humor was at an all-time low. The light sputtered to life (barely) when I depressed the switch. I was already marching back towards the fence. I assumed.

"No need to be an asshole!" she called after me, too loudly.

"Keep it down!" I stage-whispered.

She said something else – it sounded like "Cadillac" – but was cut off. I heard a light scuffling. I swung the light around, but it was all but useless and I couldn't see her. Footsteps, I thought, headed in the opposite direction. Maybe going away mad; definitely going away.

"Tommi!" I called out. "Tommi!"

Nothing. Just the wind.

Double shit.

I went after her.

At least, I *tried* to go after her. The light died entirely seconds later. I kept walking in a straight line but I was only fooling myself. I was lost.

I backtracked. Climbed a reasonably stable pile of

trash and looked around. No motion, no landmarks, no fence. Just mounds and mounds of garbage. And they were getting harder to surmount, higher, less stable. More than once I sank in well beyond my knees. Once, up my waist. I pictured myself sinking so deep that I couldn't get out, drowning in filth, choking on it. The thought made me gag, and when I happened to catch a whiff of something particularly foul at that very moment I lost it and vomited. The taste of it in my nose and mouth was actually a relief. At least it was familiar, from my days as an unskilled undergraduate drinker.

Minutes passed. Hours. I stopped worrying about getting caught and called out her name, long and loud. What of *she* had disappeared beneath a hill of garbage? Fallen? Gotten hurt? This was all my fault. At the peak of the largest hill yet I looked in every direction, couldn't get my bearings. Dark hills against a less-dark sky. Where was the fence? The office? The highway? The dump simply wasn't that big. I was in a panic, I knew, and it was effecting my judgment, maybe my perceptions. I'd be wise to sit still, wait for the light of day, stop bumbling around before I hurt myself. Tommi was probably long since home by now, in bed or taking a long bath, nursing an understandable grudge. I heard skittering nearby, caught the moon briefly illuminating tiny red eyes, affronted by my presence. Rats. Damn it. I kept moving.

Dawn came, finally, an epoch later, yellowing the sky and spilling pink across the refuse. It was still dark, but it was the sort of grey-dark you can find your way around in, and I felt a sense of relief. I climbed the highest mountain of trash I could find, an

Everest of trash, sure I'd be able to locate the exit now.

Oh god oh god oh god oh god.

How I wish I hadn't.

Because I think, if I hadn't climbed so high, I never would have seen it. Certainly, there was no suggestion, no warning. I hadn't noticed anything out of the ordinary. No unusual sounds or smells (beyond the obvious, of course), no inexplicable sense of foreboding. No *buildup*. We expect that, I think, constantly bombarded as we are with fictional narratives, books and movies and television. Regardless of quality, they're *structured*. They make sense. Real life, of course, almost never follows a three- or five-act structure, and I'm positive, even now, that if I'd turned around before I climbed that final mound of trash, I never would have known that it was even there.

It.

It loomed over the immediate area, colossal, bathed in dawn-light, crouched atop a voluminous pile of debris. How can I describe it? A massive octopus-insect, maybe, but with two arms rather than six or eight. Human arms, ending in obscenely long, multi-jointed fingers that reached down, down, wrapped protectively around its perch. Its eyes, too many to count, burrowing into me, through me, like X-rays, imparting as they penetrated my mind a sense of age measured in uncountable eons, of needs satisfactorily met and nonnegotiable. It was, I realized, the non-fanciful equivalent of a dragon, and this, this, was its hoard. Not gold and jewels but aluminum cans and plastic straws, old ball-point pens and disposable flatware. Filth and decay? No, the opposite of that. Anything that sparkled in the sun, anything shiny or pleasurably smooth and hard. Anything *permanent.* These things were its treasures, its tithe. And woe to mankind if we didn't pay.

I ran, ran. Got out, found my way out, somehow. Not that it came after me. Me, it didn't want.

I knew what it wanted.

I don't recycle anymore. And I drink all my water out of plastic bottles. I go through maybe fifty a week, even though the tap water here tastes fine. Everything goes in the trash. Everything. I base my purchases on which products have the most wasteful packaging. Those gratuitous, colorful cardboard slipcases CDs and Blu-rays come in, for absolutely no reason? A godsend. Sometimes I buy paltry knick-knacks or sale items by the cartload, just so I can throw them immediately into the trash. Beyond wasteful. Obscenely wasteful. I have to be. *We* have to be.

Gaia. Our virgin sacrifice to It.

Dream Surplus
(The Great Molasses Flood)

Andrea does not want to be awake
(There is too much laundry)
So she steals the neighborhood's dreams.
She goes from house to house,
Brings over cookies,
Asks to borrow a cup of sugar,
And when no one is looking,
She slips the dreams into her little brown purse.
Eventually she has so many dreams
She sleeps all day long,
So that dreams spill over into her room
And take root.
Shimmering, impossibly exotic plants
Sprout directly from the linoleum,
Filling the air with the sickening scent of coconuts.
In the bathroom,
Winged scorpions bump blindly against the mirror
And feast on the birth control pills.
The coffee table eats her cat.
The neighbors cannot sleep -
They have no dreams.
"This will not do," they say
As dreams spill out of Andrea's gelatinous windows.
Mailboxes dance.
An oak tree gets a degree in theoretical physics.
The sound of melting ice rents a house on the block
For 13 dollars an hour.
"I have had enough of this," says the busybody on
the corner.
"I am going to write a letter to the editor."

The Song of Gretchen

Ah, the things that can befall the lone traveler! It seems that one could quite possibly find peace on a long trip taken by oneself, but it is only fitting that once one has begun to get accustomed to the solitude, an outside agitator should appear to jolt him back to reality. So it was as I sat musing over life in a lonely way-station one night, awaiting the arrival of a coach that was to take me on the final leg of a rather long and tiring journey. I suppose I knew that the blasted coach would not be showing, given the inclement weather outside, but I was still quietly mumbling my desire to be off just as the chap I am to tell you of sat beside me.

He was an older fellow, who had a, shall we say, distinct odour about his person. He was dressed in what seemed at first to be little more than rags, although upon further examination they had actually, at least at one time, been a fine set of clothes. At first I was tempted to offer him a coin in hopes that he would leave me to my thoughts, but a sudden, roiling rumble outside assured me that the brewing storm had at last set in and that we two, along with the clerk, would be spending the night together in this dreary place.

The gentleman was silent for some time, and I began to think that he had no interest in me. But after a time he spoke, not so much to me but more to the air about us. I was then and am now sure that this individual was quite insane, yet what he said haunts my dreams still. This is the story he told...

━━━━━

"I was traveling this selfsame road years back. I was a young man then, barely twenty, and was *en route* to my parents' ancestral home, Bennet Estates, a place I had not seen since I was but a child. My Father having recently passed on, and my Mother having been gone for many years, I was one of three children left to claim their belongings. My sorrow had waned in the weeks betwixt the day the courier had arrived at my home with the news of my father's passing and the present, leaving me merely tired and hungry when the coach arrived in the wee hours of the morning. I tossed my night bag on top and boarded the carriage, already occupied by a pair of gentlemen who readily introduced themselves as one Count Bishop and one Peter Wrells. I nodded to each in turn and introduced myself. I was glad to find my company quite silent after these formalities, and was actually able to doze for some time, despite the poor condition of the road upon which we were traveling.

It was some time before I awoke, and I did so in a state of confusion, for the coach had come to a stop outside a foreboding structure, barely visible through the sheets of rain that now poured from the sky. The horses seemed skittish as a young lady appeared in the door of the building and ran – with little elegance, I must say – to the carriage. I quickly opened the side door and ushered her in. 'Thank you' she managed as she settled into the remaining seat. From outside, the driver spoke:

'The coming storm we cannot best
  Better that we put to rest.
  Down the road there lies a manse
  Where we shall bed if given chance.'

He began to whip the horses, and they trotted forward as I took in the sight of the girl before me. She was dressed in fine clothes, and had long, dark black hair that looked wonderfully full and soft. Her features were quite distinct, and her skin pale, giving her an otherworldly look as regular flashes of lightening illuminated her face. After a few moments of studying her, my mind drifted to other things, and before too much time had passed another great structure loomed before us., surrounded by a high stone wall with only one point of ingress, a great iron gate that our coachman urged his beasts through. He spoke again, very nearly shouting to be heard through the torrential downpour:

  'Here will stay your lot tonight
  To rest and leave at morning's light.
  At the door do pull the chime
  To call the master quickly nigh.'

Our driver' habit of speaking in verse truly fascinated me, I thought as I and my traveling companions approached the heavy oaken door at the front of the large stone building. One who takes the time to add such a diversion to his job is the type of person who adds flavour to life, not unlike a fine wine that compliments a meal.

There was indeed a pull-chime beside the door, and our frantic assault upon it soon aroused activity within. Presently a tired-looking gentleman appeared, garbed only in a white robe and carrying but the last dying stub of a flicking candle. Despite the lateness of the hour he was not unfriendly, and bade us enter while the coach rattled towards a coach house at the far end of the estate. The man, an older gent, listened with feigned interest as I, Count Bishop, Mr. Wrells, and the young lady, whose name was Gretchen, introduced ourselves. He then led us up an extensive flight of stairs towards the guest rooms, explaining that the master of the house was still asleep and need not be disturbed until morning. He, apparently, was merely a servant and companion to this gentleman, who dwelled here otherwise alone.

Soon we were settled, with the girl and the Count in separate rooms, and myself and Peter (as he bade I call him) sharing the third. I slid underneath the sheets fully clothed, drifting off almost immediately while Peter watched the raging storm from our window.

I know not how long I slept, but it seemed only moments later that I was awakened by a horrific scream. Peter, having nodded off in the chair by the window, fell to the floor in his hurry to rise, and we dashed as one into the hall, where the servant soon joined us. After much fumbling about in the dark, we managed to light a pair of fresh candles, and the light they cast revealed that both of the other guest rooms' doors were open. We entered Count Bishop's first, for it was undoubtedly a man's voice that had cried out, we all agreed, and as I stepped forward and held up my light, a horrid sight greeted out eyes.

There, sprawled across the bed, was the Count, quite dead. His body was covered with blood, blood and a sickening green substance with a stench as foul as any I have ever had the displeasure of experiencing. He was not clothed, and this allowed us to note that his limbs had been twisted in directions that nature had never intended. Suddenly I remembered the girl, and I turned towards her room, noting that a trail of the hideous slime snaked in that direction. Unusually concerned for her safety, I quickly entered the second bedchamber only to find it empty, save for a mass of this same putrid substance oozing from the bed and trailing out into the hallway, where, unfortunately, it petered out after a few yards.

By now the servant was quite shaken, and he excused himself to go and fetch his master. Peter and I waited patiently, my trust in his innocence in these ghastly affairs fairly justified, I felt, as I had see him tumble from his chair at the exact moment I had been aroused by the Count's cries. But after some time we grew impatient and began to wonder if we would see either servant or master in the near future. Finally, our light running out, Peter suggested we venture down the stairs and find our hosts.

Lightning flickered on the stone walls as my companion and I slowly crept down the staircase. My candle had gone out, and his was about to die as well when a ghastly smell assaulted my senses. From behind us came a slithering, wet noise, like mud flowing down the stairs above us, just as the last of Peter's flame fluttered out.

I heard a cry moments later, and a brief flash of lightning illuminated the stairwell for a split second, long enough for me to see poor Peter tumble down the stone steps. Behind me something came, but though I turned to face it, it was again too dark to see.

I found myself nearly repeating my companion's mistake, stumbling over my own feet as I fled down the irregular stairs in total darkness. I somehow managed it, and soon found myself running over a carpeted floor towards a dimly-remembered door as something unspeakable followed behind. Reaching my goal, I fell through the portal, closed it behind me, and locked it. All was quiet now, so I fumbled in the dark until I came upon a candle. Striking a piece of rock against the stone floor, I managed to light it, and found that I was in the drawing room, which, thankfully, contained a second door opposite the one I had entered through.

I sat in this room for some time, wondering whether I should attempt to backtrack through the front hall and flee out the main entrance, or try the new door before me. Logic suggested the former option, for the...thing...had to be gone by now, but fear won out, as it often does, so I slowly turned the handle of the second door and swung it open.

A hallway stretched before me, two doors immediately discernible to one side. I began to move forward, intending to escape through a servant's entrance and steal the coach outside, but a sound from behind the first door gave me pause. At first I thought it was surely the...thing, but when the low moan again issued forth I recognized it as the sound of a human being. I carefully opened the door, holding my candle high to illuminate as much of the room as possible. It was a small bedroom, and sprawled across the bed was Gretchen, coated with that same sickening slime but seemingly unharmed. I set my candle down and began to wipe the vile stuff from her as she seemed to awaken as if from a daze.

'We must leave this place,' I began, 'the master of this house is some beast...' But my words were cut off as she suddenly...kissed me. She drew me to her breast and began to disrobe, wiping the slime from her body with her discarded clothing. I looked into her eyes, eyes that were green and evil. Somehow, though, I did not care, not even when her arms began to grow long and leathery did I pull away from her otherwise luscious body. She held me ever tighter, began to crush my bones, but in doing so she toppled us both, accidentally upturning the table on which I had set my light source. The candle fell, igniting a puddle of slime that was pooling on the floor. It burned quickly, like oil, and the Gretchen-Thing howled in terror and released me, stumbling about on protrusions that were half leg and half...something else. Her arms – now tentacles – flailed madly about her head as the flame raced along the trail of muck she left behind, and, despite my efforts, it caught her. I threw myself upon her as her form reverted, became more and more human in appearance, trying in vain to extinguish the flames because I desired her more than anything on this Earth, even as she tried to kill me, I desired her!"

━━━━━

At this point the old man grabbed my collar, bellowing "I desired her!" and shaking me until, with the help of the astounded clerk, I managed to pry him off. The clerk ejected him into the storm and apologized profusely, though the damage to my bodily self was negligible. But the damage to my soul... I dream now of this tale every night, and my passion for the creature the mad stranger described only grows with each nocturnal vision. Soon, I will seek her out. She still lives, I know this to be true. Soon...

This One's For the Dandelions, the Clover, the Watercress

"And, er, how did you know my mother again?" The strange man had already worked his foot into the door, in case Jack tried to close it. Like an old-school encyclopedia salesman. "She didn't have any money you know." A lot of peripherals and heretofore unknown relatives had descended upon the house since the old woman's passing. Communicating that she'd died broke generally sent them scampering.

"Oh I know that, that I know," replied the man. He was an odd duck, this one. His look was defiantly out of date, his suit, overcoat, and fedora too precisely rumpled. To say nothing of his practiced, theatrical demeanor. He came off as some sort of genre caricature, although Jack was hard-pressed to precisely identify the character type. Or even the genre.

"It's getting late," Jack said. Indeed, the sky was red, the sun just a lip of gold peeping over the horizon.

"Please, this will only take a moment of your time," the odd man persisted. "I'll be out of your *hair* before dark." He grinned as he said this, as if it were particularly clever.

"All right, all right," Jack acquiesced. The man slithered in before he could open the door another inch, as if he'd always had the ability to do so and was just waiting for the invitation.

"Arnie Hoffstetter," the man said, extending a

hand. Jack reluctantly shook it.

"You... knew my mother?" Jack repeated. He cringed inwardly, half resigned to the idea that this strange person was about to reveal that he'd been the old woman's lover, or something equally appalling.

"Not as such, as such," Arnie Hoffstetter said, looking eagerly around. As if he expected to discover some sort damning clue. A smoking gun.

"A neighbor, then?"

"Oh, we're all neighbors, Mr. Lepus. It is Mr. Lepus, isn't it?" He rather brazenly strode into the living room proper, head darting this way and that. There wasn't much to see aside from packing boxes, many already sealed with tape, containing the old woman's former belongings. Her personal treasures, stripped of context and meaning in the space of a single breath. Hoffstetter lifted the flap of one of the unsealed boxes and peered curiously inside.

"Mr. Lepus, yes," Jack said. "I decided to keep my maiden name when I married." When Hoffstetter didn't respond to the gag he added , reluctantly, "You can call me Jack."

"Oh, you're married?" Hoffstetter asked, in the manner someone asks when they don't really care, and are just making sounds to prompt your next response.

"It was a joke," Jack said.

"Uh huh." Hoffstetter poked his head into the kitchen, sniffed the air. Jack glanced nervously out the window. It was getting late now, dusk deep and thick. This weirdo had to go.

"What, exactly, is it I can do for you?" he asked, pointedly.

"Well, right down to business. I like that in a man.

No dallying. Why I..."

"Your point, Mr. Hoffstetter," Jack said, rearing up to his full height (five foot six *and a half*) and crossing his arms.

"Of course, of course," Hoffstetter said. He looked Jack right in the eye. "I understand... Well, I understand that your mother owned a..." here he paused dramatically "...*rabbit*." He flinched, as if from some anticipated reaction on Jack's part.

"Yeah," Jack said. Hoffstetter was instantly flustered, as if he'd expected Jack to fly off the handle, or at least deny it.

"So you *admit*..."

"Yeah, she had a house rabbit. As a pet."

"Because I can smell it, you know," Hoffstetter went on. Like he'd crafted his response to Jack's anticipated denial meticulously, and wasn't about to waste it, even though Jack hadn't denied anything. "They have a very distinct smell. Vile." He shook his head.

"Did you, er, want the rabbit?" Jack asked. "Because I already gave him away."

"So you admit it was a male?" Hoffstetter replied, head canted, eyes narrowed. He took an accusatory step towards Jack.

"She always called it 'he', so I assumed. I don't know if he was fixed, though. Maybe you could track him down and check for yourself."

"And where did this supposed *house rabbit* come from?" Hoffstetter pressed.

"What, exactly, is your interest in all this, Mr Hoffstetter?"

"Let's just say it's in the interests of... the community."

Jack frowned. This had gone on long enough. Too long.

"I really have to ask you to..." he began.

"Leave?" the bizarre man finished for him.

"Yes." A nervous glance at the window, dark now. Hoffstetter followed his gaze.

"Something wrong?" the intruder asked.

"Hard to believe anyone could be that un-self-aware," Jack responded.

"How droll," Hoffstetter said.

They stared at each other for a long minute.

"You've been staying here?" Hoffstetter finally asked. "With your mother?"

"Yes." They'd crossed a line. Rounded a corner. Entered a no-bullshit zone. All cards on the table.

"For how long? Ten months, I'd gather."

"About that, yes."

"And how did she die again? If you don't mind my asking."

"She had a heart attack."

"I see. Lucky her."

"Yes. Lucky."

"Did something startling, perhaps, bring on this... heart attack?" Hoffstetter had that sly look again.

"No," Jack said coolly. "I wasn't even home."

"I see."

This time, they both glanced out the window, simultaneously. The full moon was just visible over the trees lining the far side of the road.

"And there it is," Hoffstetter said quietly. Almost a whisper.

"And here we are," Jack responded. He was unbuttoning his shirt.

"Warm, Mr. Lepus? It doesn't seem particularly

warm in here. To me."

"Just getting comfortable," Jack said, tossing the shirt aside. He kicked off his shoes.

"Ah. *Changing* into something more comfortable."

"You might say that. If you were a raging hack comedian."

"Can't land 'em all, Mr. Lepus. You can't land them all." Reaching into his overcoat, Hoffstetter slowly extracted a long, narrow object that looked like a miniature baseball bat. A Mexican war club.

It was plated in pure silver.

Jack was taking off his pants.

"I'm waiting," he said, indicating the silver club. He was completely naked now.

"Oh I would never," Hoffstetter said. "Not yet. That would be... murder."

"Assault at best, with that little thing," Jack said, again indicating the club.

"I could say the same," Hoffstetter said, indicating a particular aspect of Jack's anatomy. "But the time for jokes is past."

"Indeed."

They waited, in silence, another minute or so.

Then it happened.

Jack doubled over, clearly in agony. He cried out as his bones cracked and broke and melded and reformed, hair sprouting from his body, teeth lengthening, fingernails toughening and extending and curving into claws.

Painful seconds later, Jack Lepus the man was gone.

Before Arnie Hoffstetter crouched that most despicable of supernatural terrors –

The wererabbit.

Lunging forward, striking before the tiny creature could scamper away, Arnie Hoffstetter pummeled it to death with the silver-plated war club. A true death, because silver was a were-creature's sole weakness.

Wiping the club clean on the living room curtains, Arnie admired his handiwork for a moment before quickly making his exit. Best to be well away when the authorities arrived. Yet he paused, briefly, in the front yard, casting his eyes downward at the lawn. Kentucky bluegrass, interspersed with the occasional dandelion.

"You're safe, now," he told them.

Then he quickly and dramatically marched to the end of the block. His Uber driver had grown impatient and left, but he could summon another.

The war continued.

The Stroll

Keith was taking a study break when he saw them. He'd only glanced outside for a moment, but there was no missing a crowd of that size. He approached the window, shielding his eyes from the late morning sun. There were hundreds – perhaps a thousand – individuals making their way down Birch Street, westbound, into town, and as they moved easily along more and more people joined them; from behind, from side streets and alleys, and out of his neighbors' houses the people poured. A few trotted to catch up, but most were lazily absorbed and quickly fell into step with the leisurely-proceeding throng.

Where the hell are they all going? he wondered first. *Christ, did something happen?* next. He leaned as far out of his second-story window as he dared, looking first in the direction the crown was headed, then in the one they had come from. There were no sirens, he saw no glow of fire, no chaos, nothing out of the ordinary. And everyone seemed so calm. Stepping away from the window he located the remote and flipped on the television, quickly scanning the local channels for signs of trouble. Again, nothing. What was going on? Half certain that he'd been hallucinating, he looked out the window again, but they were still there, a river of human beings fed by tributaries at every street, every door.

"Hey!" Keith yelled down to no one in particular, "Hey – what's going on? Hey!" No one stopped, but a few people – those near enough to hear him – looked up. Someone, Keith couldn't see who, cried out:

"Come on!" Another:

"Hurry up!"

So he bolted down the stairs, not because he was afraid he'd miss them – the crowd seemed endless – but simply to satisfy his curiosity all the sooner. He burst out the front door and suddenly stopped, almost in awe. There were so many: small children with their parents, senior citizens, college students like himself, men, women, blacks, whites, Asians, Hispanics... Some of them were dressed like they'd just walked out of work, right off the job. Others were more casual. A few wore suits. At least one Keith saw was naked.

"Where is everyone going?" he called out again. A few people nearby smiled in his direction and one, a girl, reached out and lightly took his hand.

"Come on," she said, "you have to come with us." He let her lead him into the mass.

The going was slow and easy, everyone moving amicably along at a casual stroll. Others still joined in from either side, slowly pushing Keith towards the middle, but he wasn't crowded. It was quite pleasant, in fact. From his window the people had seemed like cattle, moving inexorably forward, but here, in the crowd, everyone laughed and talked, smiled and joked. Keith met a number of people as they walked, shared stories with them, shared fears and hopes. Someone was passing around a cooler filled with cans of soda and he took one. Later someone passed around a bottle of whiskey, and he took a drink from that, too.

It was twilight by the time he caught hold of himself. He looked around, trying to figure out where they might be, but there were just too many people. He had had such a good time – it was like a traveling party – but he was tired now, so tired. And he suddenly remembered why he'd come down from his studies in the first place. "Where are we going, anyway?" he asked an elderly man next to him.

"What?" the man asked. There were two other elderly men – in their seventies, at least – making a lot of noise nearby; they were drunk.

"Going," repeated Keith. "Where are we going?"

"Why," the man answered, "we're going to the place where you get old."

"Where you get old?" Keith didn't understand.

"You, me, all of us. Where we get old."

"But I'm not even twenty-one yet," Keith protested. "I just started college. I was studying for midterms. I..." But as he gestured he saw his hands, his claw-like, withered hands. A stab of arthritic pain shot up his arms as he clenched his fists. "No!!" he screamed , "I'm not old yet! I'm not!!"

People continued to join from either side, and the crowd moved forward, ever forward.

The Phone

It was stealing, Jonah couldn't deny that. But, well, it was justified.

The gas pumps looked like antiques. He imagined the *American Pickers* guys losing their minds if they came across them. He wasn't even sure they were real, or functional, rather, but he was coasting on fumes so he'd pulled in and, surprise surprise, they were legit. On the porch of the little store – of course there was a little store, and of course it had a porch – two characters (there was no other way to describe them) watched as he pumped. They seemed disappointed that he hadn't looked in vain for a credit card slot first, or done something equally boneheaded. Seated in sun-faded lawn chairs, they were old but not yet ancient, sipping beers out of cans that looked like they'd been fished out of an abandoned well. One of them had a piece of straw stuck in his teeth, which he chewed on absently and drank around expertly.

"So. Cash only?" he called out to the men.

"Got Square if'n all you got's a card," answered one of them. The one chewing on the piece of straw. He managed a sip from his beer simultaneously. Multitasking.

"Got a ker-chunker too, if you're one a' them folks what don't trust the Internet," the other one added.

Ker-chunker? Did he mean a credit card imprinter? Jonah hadn't seen one of those clunky things since he was a child.

"It's okay, I've got cash," he said. He pumped twenty bucks exactly, the extent of said cash.

"Cash is the way to go," nodded the first man. The second man snorted.

"*Gold* is the way to go," the second man declared, and it had the feel of a perpetual argument between the two.

They were interrupted by the near yet distant jangle of an old-school telephone. Did the first man pale slightly, or was it just a trick of the light?

"Mercy God, not again..." the second man quickly said.

The phone rang again, not from inside, or from a pocket, but somewhere behind Jonah. He turned around. Across the street, a pay phone, an honest-to-god *pay phone*. As if he didn't already feel like he'd driven into the past.

"You stay away from that phone, mister," one of the old men told him. Jonah was halfway to them, his wallet out. He stepped onto the porch, twenty in hand, but neither man reached for it. They were both staring past him, at the phone.

"Okay," Jonah said. "What's the gag?"

"No gag, mister. That phone, she's a killer."

"Killer phone. Right."

The man locked eyes with him. The ringing had stopped.

"I ain't playing, here. You answer that phone, you die. It's a damned fact."

The other old man nodded sagely.

"You don't say," Jonah said, frowning.

"It's facts," the first man reiterated. "The first time it happened was in 1965. My family bought the place in '60. Phone was out of service even then. Far as we knew, it hadn't worked in years, if ever. Then one day it starts ringing and ringing and ringing. My pop, he figures, well, maybe they fixed the damn thing and are running a test, you know? So he strolls across the highway and picks up the receiver and is all 'Hello? Hello?' And then he listens, and his face goes white as a sheet and he starts hollerin'. 'No!' he shouts, 'I ain't never heard of no such!' I'll never forget them words, or the way he said 'em, neither. Like his brain was coming apart at the seams. Then he keels over, stone dead, just like that. Stroke, they said. Ten-year-old me got up the nerve, maybe a week later, to pick up that receiver and listen, but there wasn't nothing there. Not even a dial tone."

"That phone straight-up killed Sam's pappy," Ed said. "That phone or something on the other end of it."

"If all this is true," Jonah said slowly, "then I'm real sorry about your... pappy. But it must have been a coincidence. People see and hear all sorts of crazy shi– *things* when they suffer a stroke."

"Uh-huh," Sam agreed. "Smell 'em, too. But this wasn't that. Know that for a fact.

"Because it happened again.

"About ten years later, as I recall," Sam declared. Ed nodded in agreement. "I was pretty much running the place on my own – my ma, she didn't carry on so well after Pappy died – and we was full-service back in those days, even though, by then, the move was away from that. I was topping off a little foreign job when that old phone suddenly starts ringing. Damn near gave *me* a stroke, and I was a young man then. Guy who owned the car, he'd been inside, buying a couple of cokes. He come out and, kind of joking around, says to his wife, who's in the passenger seat with the window rolled down, he says to her 'Well let's see who it is!' and marches over there. I don't know why I didn't say anything; maybe I wanted to see what would happen, maybe I was hopin' nothing would. I just stood there, watching as he walked over and picked up that receiver. 'Speaking,' he says, first thing. Having fun with whoever was on the other end. But then he listens for a second and suddenly he starts screaming, just screaming his head off like he's losing his mind or being tortured alive or maybe both at once. Then blood starts running down his neck and at first I couldn't figure out where it was coming from but then I realized that it was coming out of his *ears*. He topples over, right there in the road. Dead as a post."

"And he weren't the last," Ed said. "Every once in a while, no pattern, that phone rings. And whoever picks it up dies or goes crazy or both. I seen it myself, twice since I come on. I called the phone company, told them the thing was no good and to come out here and fix it or pull it out, but they insist there *ain't* no phone here, never has been."

"Sometimes," Sam said, his eyes taking on a faraway look, "I think about getting myself a baseball bat and just waling the tar out o' that thing. Blowing it up. Backing over it with the tow truck..." he sighed.

"Scared," Ed explained. "Not that I blame him."

"I wonder, sometimes, if maybe God's on the other end of that line," Sam said quietly. "Whisperin' the secrets of the universe. Only our regular-person brains, they can't handle it. We just ain't ready yet."

"This is..." Jonah began, but only got that far when the phone began to ring again.

Brrriiinnng!

Jonah turned, stared at it. The old men's story was absurd.

Brrriiinnng!

And yet.

Brrriiinnng!

He'd taken three full steps before he even realized what he was doing.

"Don't do it!" one of the old men said, but with no real gravitas.

"Whatever it's got to say, you don't want to hear it!" the other one called after him.

He ignored them.

Brrriiinnng!

Glancing both ways, he slowly crossed the highway.

Brrriiinnng!

His hand was on the receiver. He hesitated.

Brrriiinnng! Brrriiinnng!

Last chance. Walk away. Walk away...

...and never know.

He couldn't.

Brrriiinnng! Brrriiinnng! Brrriiinnng!

He lifted the receiver, cutting off the last ring. Slowly, he raised it to his ear.

"Hello?" he said. Just above a whisper. His hands were shaking.

Silence, then—

"Mateo?"

"W-what?" Jonah asked.

"Is *Mateo* there? Fool, I been callin' all *day*. Is that punk-ass *vato* there, or what? Do I even got the right number? Hello? Hello?"

He turned and looked back across the highway, to

where the two old men were laughing so hard that they could barely breathe. One of them had fallen out of his chair.

It was then and there that Jonah decided not to pay for his gas. It was stealing, he couldn't deny that. But damn it, it was justified.

Dog in the Morning Meeting

A dog was running up and down the wall,
Defying gravity and trying everyone's patience.
"Get that dog out of here," said someone,
"We're trying to hold a meeting."
They opened the door, but the dog did not run out.
"Get a broom," said Marcia from purchasing,
"When something like this happens, you should
always get a broom."
They got a broom and hit the dog,
But it scampered onto the ceiling.
"We are never going to get any work done," said Barry,
"Who let that dog in here, anyway?"

Ghost of a Scene

"Here?" Carol asked, a bit put off. "Why would Jeremy want to hang out *here?* Why would anyone ever hang out *here?*"

"Maybe it was different ten years ago," her husband suggested.

"Oh, Phil, it's an industrial park. How different could it have been?"

"It wasn't any different, not on the outside," said the man in the backseat. He was tall, slim, precise, his suit immaculate if somewhat out of style. Grey hair, short, neatly trimmed. Narrow, waxed mustache in the imperial style. Phil found this latter affectation particularly contrived.

"He's what my father used to call 'a real character'," he'd told Carol the first time she'd brought the fellow around. "Which meant that my father thought the person in question was either an asshole or a complete idiot."

"He's an urban mage," she'd explained.

"What?"

"He understands *arcane* things," she'd insisted. "He'll be able to help us. You'll see."

"Help us? Help us with what, for Christ's sake?"

"I just want to *see* him Phil. One last time"

Phil put the sedan in P and turned off the ignition. The night was clear and crisp-cold, the silence all-encompassing. "That's why it was set up here," the man in the backseat said. "No one comes here. No cops, no outsiders. No poseurs. These subcultures tend to be very insular."

They got out of the car.

"Which one?" Phil asked.

The urban mage closed his eyes and touched his right temple with the first two fingers of his right hand. After several seconds his left arm rose, seemingly of its own accord, and began to slowly sweep back and forth. A moment later he was pointing at one dreary block of windowless building in particular.

"There," he said quietly. "It was there. Bands, and sometimes a DJ. Dancing. BYOB. Some drugs but nothing too heavy. It wasn't a heavy drug scene."

"What's BYOB?" asked Carol.

"Oh, really, Carol..." Phil said, rolling his eyes.

"I really don't know!" she snapped.

The mage turned to them, speaking slowly and deliberately.

"We can go in, all of us," he told them. "All the way, if you like."

"How is that possible?" asked Phil. He was the more skeptical of the two.

"These... *scenes*," the mage explained, "are organic, as organic as any complex system. People drift in and out, rise to dominance, outgrow whatever need the scene fulfilled in their lives and move on. But the scene itself, it remains, constantly growing and changing. A living thing." He paused. Rather theatrically, Phil thought. "Until it isn't. And like any living thing, any *formerly* living thing..."

"So scenes die?" Carol asked. "Like people?" She was endlessly fascinated by his performance.

"Well you don't see a lot of mods or greasers around anymore, do you?" Phil said irritably. How did she ever talk him into this?

"Come," said the mage.

They followed.

The outside of the low, concrete slab of building had been tagged with graffiti, gang symbols as incomprehensible as a string of ancient runes. Isolated tufts of tenacious, brown grass had forced their way up through cracks in the asphalt, and there was a scattering of litter. The summer-haze sun had just begun to dip below a taller, wider building situated to their rear, smearing the parking lot in shadow. "I should get the flashlight," Phil said. "I've got one in the trunk," he explained to the mage. "It's a good one. Fifteen thousand lumens."

"Oh, you and your lumens." Carol waved his foolishness away.

"We won't need it," the mage said. They stood before a steel door now, solid, industrial, the only entrance on this side of the building. The mage placed the back of his hand against it, as one does before opening a door during a fire. Then, closing his eyes, he touched the knob lightly. "Locked," he whispered to himself. "Locked *now*, but not *then*..." He ran a finger lightly around the knob. Once. Twice. Three times.

Phil frowned. Nice bit of stagecraft, there. Almost obfuscated the fact that Mr. Mage hadn't actually attempted the knob in the first place. He was about to point this out when he suddenly cocked his head, listening.

"Do you hear that?" he asked Carol.

She did, barely. Music. Raucous, undisciplined.

Rock music. Or what passed for rock music these days. Give her the Smashing Pumpkins, or Pearl Jam. But then it was gone, leaving behind the impression of a fleeting memory more than real sounds, actually heard.

The mage turned the knob and the door opened.

Cigarette smoke and sweat, just for an instant. Then these odors were gone, replaced by the stale smell of abandonment and dust. The space beyond the door was entirely open, like a warehouse, dimly visible in the sunlight leaking through six yellowed, equidistant skylights. Re-purposed electrical lights of all shapes and sizes hung from the ceiling, including several table lamps, their cords draped over pipes, taped to the ceiling, running every which way in a bewildering web. At the far end, a low, hastily constructed stage that, even empty, threatened to collapse at any moment. Three gutted refrigerators. Distressed folding chairs and pilfered lawn furniture, lightly rusted. Beer cans and bottles everywhere - dead soldiers. A huge glass jar sat upon a cheap aluminum-plastic banquet table in front of the refrigerators. A piece of paper was taped to the jar, the tape yellow with time. "~~TIPS~~ TITS" the paper read.

"Reminds me of college," Phil said, almost smiling.

"I don't know what kind of college *you* went to," Carol said coolly.

"Three chairs, please, Phil," said the mage. "Quickly, before we lose the light."

Phil collected three serviceable folding chairs and set them up in a rough circle. Carol dusted hers off with a Kleenex fished out of her purse before sitting down.

"We don't need a Ouija board or anything?" Phil asked, only half joking. He pronounced it *weejee*.

"Nothing so jejune," the mage said, taking his seat.

"Do we hold hands?" Carol asked.

"Only if Phil wants to," the mage said, favoring her husband with a lascivious wink.

Fucking smartass, Phil thought.

The mage closed his eyes, mumbled something in a foreign language, and then spoke, in English, in a loud, clear voice.

"Come to us! We know you are still here! Lingering, never entirely forgotten by those who created you and who perpetuated you and who lived at your center and also at your fringes. Who needed you and loved you. Who you accepted and perhaps even rejected. We wish to see you. We wish to experience you and offer you this opportunity to relive your glories." He paused here, as if waiting for a response. "Are you there?"

"I'm sorry, no one can take your call right now..." Phil whispered. Carol slapped him on the knee.

"Are your eyes closed?" the mage asked.

"No."

"Yes," Carol said, quickly closing them.

"Close them, then."

Sighing, Phil closed his eyes as well.

The first sensation wasn't a sound, or a smell. It was tactile. A sort of vibration, dull and regular. It was the music again, felt before it was heard. Slowly it faded in, like a radio being carefully tuned to the right channel. Cigarette smoke, bodies, spilled beers, a sense of motion all around them. Voices, intertwined and indistinct, but loud, louder, raised to be heard over the music. Something jostled Carol and she gasped.

Phil heard it, clear as day.

"Sorry, lady."

He opened his eyes.

People, mostly but not exclusively young. Drinking, talking, smoking, flirting. Leather and fishnets and boots and band tees and wild hair and defiantly conservative hair and and...

There was a band on the stage, tearing through a number that was equal parts country and gothic rock and good old fashioned rock 'n' roll. Visually, the performers looked like David Bowie Day at the Brewster County Fair.

"Holy shit," Phil said. Carol opened her eyes at the sound of his voice.

"Oh, my," she said. Phil turned to the mage.

"You, you took us back in time?" he asked, flabbergasted. The slim man shook his head.

"No, we haven't gone anywhere. Look closely."

The crazy bastard was right. The undeniable solidity Phil first perceived was, indeed, illusory. He could see *through* the people around them, but only when he concentrated, when he really tried. One of them caught him staring and gave him a dirty look. Phil quickly looked away.

"They're not really here," the mage said, leaning over and speaking directly into Phil's ear in order to be heard over the hubbub. "We are, essentially, *inside* a ghost."

"These are all ghosts?" Carol asked, awed.

"Not just the people, everything. Look, look at the lights."

The beaten and battered lamps and bulbs that hung from the ceiling were newer now, in working order, lit up and filling the space with dim, bar-level light. But through them, behind them, the "real" character of the lights was still visible. Dust-covered. Inoperative.

"Don't try too hard to perceive the reality behind the illusion," the mage warned her, "or you'll tumble right out of it, break the spell."

Carol nodded.

"Can we... talk to them?"

The mage nodded.

"Interact with them any way that you please. They may acknowledge you, they may not. A small few may not be able to perceive you, so keep that in mind. If someone ignores you entirely, they're not necessarily being obstinate."

Phil stood, slowly. Being here, in a place like this, even if it was a phantasmagoria, made him feel like a kid again. He grinned.

"I'm gonna get a drink!" he said. "Can I do that?" he asked the mage. The slim man shrugged. Why not?

"Phil, really! Don't forget why we're here!" But he was already halfway across the room.

The three refrigerators behind the banquet table were packed with beers now, so many that they had been stacked horizontally, necks out. The TITS jar was stuffed with paper money and some change. Two young girls in tight shirts and fishnets were selling the beers for two dollars each.

"What have you got?" Phil asked one of the girls.

"Bud," she said.

"Just Bud?"

"What did you expect, dad? Two bucks."

"Did you just call me dad? Like daddy-o?"

"Dad like you're old enough to be my fucking dad. Two bucks."

Phil handed her a crisp new five. The girl passed him a beer and threw his balled-up change into the TITS jar without asking.

"This tastes kind of flat and bland," Phil noted, returning to the others. "Is that part of it?" he asked the mage.

"It's a Budweiser," the mage responded.

Everyone's a comedian, Phil thought.

Carol was craning her neck, looking around eagerly.

"Do you think he's really here?" she asked no one in particular. "Oh I hope he's here!"

"Remember, it won't actually be him," the mage reminded her, "not even his ghost, really. These people you see, probably most of them are still alive."

"So what we're seeing here, it's the ghost of a *place*," Phil said.

"Not of a place. Of... a moment in time. But, understand, not a *specific* moment. An amalgamation. That is why it's possible, even likely, that your Mr. Billings will be here."

"Excuse me, do you know Jeremy Billings?" Carol asked, accosting a passerby. The girl shook her head and quickly moved on.

"Might want to be a bit more subtle," the mage gently suggested.

"They probably think we're cops," Phil said, absently sipping his flat ghost beer. He wondered if his three dollars would still be in the TITS jar when they came out of this, crumpled and dusty with age. What about the fiver? Had it been supernaturally transported to the past when he gave it to that girl in the tight shirt? If so, did anyone back then notice that it was a little off, the date printed on it a decade in the future? His mind reeled.

Carol was roaming around now, looking for her brother. The band wrapped up their current song with an extended flourish. "We're taking a break but we'll be right back!" the lead singer said into his mic. "We're Diabetic Napalm," the guitarist quickly added, almost an afterthought.

Phil turned his chair around and sat down next to the mage. His beer was getting hard to hold, his fingers simultaneously slipping off of and sinking into the glass.

"You're dropping out already," the mage said, noting this. "You've no attachment to this place. It's an irrelevancy to you so you're unconsciously dismissing it."

Phil looked after Carol. It's not like he didn't feel her pain, didn't understand.

"She'll last a little longer," the mage said. "She does have an attachment, peripheral though it may be."

"Jeremy," Phil nodded. He automatically raised the beer bottle to his lips but it was gone. Everything was gone and for an instant he thought he'd been struck blind. But no, he was just sitting alone, in a dark, deserted building.

Well, not quite alone, wisps of darker shadow moved through the darkness all around him, humanoid, indistinct. Then they too faded.

"Hello?" he said into the darkness.

"I'm here." The mage.

"Where's Carol? Did she find him? Did she get to

see Jeremy?" It was pitch black now that the sun had gone down, and he was afraid to stand up much less try to find the exit. He'd probably break his neck.

"Wait," the mage said.

They waited. A minute. Two. Longer. Still longer, until time became meaningless.

"It's been at least an hour," Phil said. He was worried now.

"It's only been ten minutes," the mage sighed. "Still too long." A flame flared into life; a cigarette lighter. The mage stood, using it to light his way. "We should go."

"But where's Carol?" Phil insisted. "Where's my wife?"

"I'm afraid she found him," the mage said. He carefully made his way to the outside door, but Phil didn't follow.

"What do you mean?" he shouted, panic setting in. "Where is she, you crazy fuck? Don't walk away from me! *Where is she?* **Where's my wife???**"

Oblique

"Taa-daa!" Professor Oblique said, dramatically whipping the sheet off the red, 1987 Yugo.

"Really, Abner?" said Professor Yu. "You actually went with the Yugo?"

"What choice did I have?" Oblique snapped, instantly irritated. "They've been particularly niggardly with funding since that chaos at the sorority house..."

"Yes, yes, we know all about it," Doctor Prowse said, waving a dismissive hand. "And you shouldn't say *niggardly*."

"Whyever not?" Oblique demanded in a huff. "It's not a bad word! Its etymology is entirely separate from the racial slur you're thinking of!"

"Yes," Prowse said, "but not everybody knows that."

"And I should take everyone else's ignorance into account whenever I speak? I'd be a mute!"

That might not be so bad, Yu thought to herself.

"Well, thank you for the diversion, anyway, Professor. I can't speak for Professor Yu, but I have a syllabus to update."

The two instructors let themselves out.

"I'd rattle my fist and declare them fools," Oblique sighed, "but that seems ever so stereotypical."

"But the Time Yugo really works, right Doc?" asked Emily.

"I've asked you not to call me 'Doc'," he told his student aide. "But yes, it works, in large part because there is nothing, *nothing* that demands we move only one direction in time. It's akin to suggesting that you can walk east to west across a room, but not west to east."

"So going back in time is as easy as walking across the room?"

"*Backward* in time, and yes. Easier, actually. Theoretically, it should be no different than moving *forward* in time, which we do constantly, without even trying. In fact, for all we know we *are* going backward. Maybe broken glass should spontaneously reform, leaves leap back onto the trees as autumn winds to an opening and segues into summer. And so on and so forth. I'm being a tad facetious, but you get the idea."

"Show me," Emily said coyly, rocking back and forth on the tips of her toes, her hands clasped behind her back. This usually got her what she wanted. Especially when she was wearing her too-short cutoff jean shorts, like she was today.

"Well..." Professor Oblique said, stroking his non-existent beard. "I don't suppose a short jaunt would do any harm. And you have been invaluable to me this semester..."

"Two sugars in your coffee, I always remembered," Emily agreed.

"Okay. Let's do it!"

2

"I think I'd like to see Ancient Rome," Emily said as she climbed into the passenger seat. "Or meet Vanilla Ice." She automatically tried to put her seat belt on, forgetting that this was a Yugo. Of course it didn't work.

"Well, we won't be doing any of that," Professor Oblique said. "It would be far too irresponsible of me to go prancing about time and space with one of my students in tow. We'll just take a quick jaunt, just far enough back to impress upon you that it works." Emily pouted, another maneuver that often got her what she wanted. But Professor Oblique didn't notice.

"Okay," he said. "Are you ready?"

"Energize!" Emily said.

"I don't know what that means!" Professor Oblique admitted as he turned the key to start the little car. It vibrated to life. He depressed the clutch and struggled the shoddy transmission into reverse.

"That's all you have to do?" Emily asked.

"This is time travel, young lady, not rocket science."

There was a low pop, their stomachs dropped, and everything around them smeared into a kaleidoscope of color, just for an instant.

"Hooray!" Emily said, clapping her hands.

They stepped out of the Time Yugo, which was on the opposite side of the room now, and found themselves face-to-face with... themselves.

3

"Taa-daa!" Professor Oblique said.

"You fool!" the other Professor Oblique said. He was standing next to a duplicate of the Time Yugo, one still covered with the sheet. A duplicate of Emily stood next to him, her jaw denting the floor.

"Neat!" said Emily. She gave her other self the once-over. "I have even nicer legs than I thought."

"You fool!" the other Oblique repeated. "Doctor Prowse and Professor Yu will be here any moment! You'll undermine my dramatic unveiling entirely! And who's this girl?"

"Uh, that's me," both Emilys said simultaneously.

"Oh, relax, Abner," Oblique said. "This will be even better."

"But the attention will all be on you!" the other Oblique lamented. "*And*, and, you're... you're likely to create a paradox!"

"Paradox, schmeradox. That's just a theory."

The lab door opened.

"Professor Oblique, Professor Oblique," Doctor Prowse nodded to each Oblique in turn as he stepped into the room.

"*Two* Professor Obliques?" Professor Yu frowned. "Terrific."

"As if any more proof were necessary that my Time Yugo is fully functional!" the Oblique from the future beamed.

"I have to give it to you," Doctor Prowse said, extending his hand to the future Oblique. "You've proved a lot of people wrong."

"You owe me a dollar," Yu reminded Prowse.

"Professor Oblique, I'd like to buy you a drink!" Prowse said.

"He takes two sugars," said Emily.

"This is unconscionable!" the other Oblique fumed. "*He's* raking in the accolades and free drinks, while I stand here, completely ignored! Who does he think he is?"

"Er..." said the other Emily.

The other Oblique tore the sheet off his Time Yugo and climbed inside. "I'm going to teach him a lesson he won't soon regret!" he declared.

"**For**get," the other Emily corrected him. Then, "Can I come?"

"No!" shouted the other Oblique, shifting the car into reverse.

4

A third Time Yugo shimmer-popped into existence, moments before Prowse and Yu entered the room. Yet another Professor Oblique hopped out, immediately confronting the previously intruding Oblique.

"Now see here...!" he began, poking Oblique in the chest with his finger.

"You can't talk that way to Professor Oblique!" Emily said.

"I'll speak to *Abner* here any way I choose, young lady! Who are you, anyway?"

Emily fumed.

"I suggest you return from whence you came!" Professor Oblique said. "I have the situation fully in hand!"

"You most certainly do not!" the newest Oblique snarled. "I demand that you return to the future immediately!"

"And *I* demand that *you* return to the future immediately!" Oblique countered.

"Fight! Fight! Fight!" the other Emily chanted.

"This is a fiasco!" the other Oblique lamented. "I'll be a laughing stock if Doctor Prowse and Professor Yu walk into this! Quick," he told his Emily, "lock the door." She scampered over to the lab door and threw the bolt.

A fourth Time Yugo appeared and still another

159

Professor Oblique tumbled out of it, near panic.

"Unlock that door, quickly!" he shouted. A third Emily climbed out of the passenger seat and waved to the other two.

"You need to return to the future immediately!" two of the established Obliques demanded, not quite simultaneously.

"There's no time to argue!" this latest Oblique shouted. "You must unlock that door immediately!"

5

"Who are you to gallivant through time, barking orders?" the original Oblique demanded.

"I'm *you*," the latest Oblique said, indicating the original Oblique specifically. "In approximately sixty seconds you're going to realize the error inherent in locking that door and travel back in time in order to prevent it!"

The original Oblique crossed his arms and adopted a most stubborn demeanor.

"In that case, I refuse to take any such action."

"You must! In fact you will, because I'm here now and I'm you!"

"We're all him!" the other two Obliques said.

"I won't. Your timeline is hereby cut off."

"Are we going to die?" the latest Emily asked, wringing her hands.

"No," said the latest Oblique.

"Yes," said the other Oblique.

"Maybe," said the no-longer-newest Oblique.

"It doesn't matter," said the original Oblique.

"She's too pretty to die!" interjected the original Emily.

160

"Thank you!" said the latest Emily.

The other Oblique raised his hands in the air.

"Listen to me! You all need to go back where you came from!" he said.

"Racist," mumbled the original Emily. The latest Emily, meanwhile, was taking a head count. She counted twice, triple-checking her math on her fingers, and then started screaming.

"There's four Professor Obliques and only three of me!" she shrieked. "I did die! I mean, I do die! I did! I do! I will!"

"Now see what you've done!" the other Oblique groaned.

"Will you please calm down, you hysterical female?" the no-longer-newest Oblique snapped.

"That's even more racist!" the other Emily said.

"It's *sexist*, and no it isn't!" the Oblique in question countered.

"Also, *Professors Oblique* would be the proper nomenclature," the latest Oblique interjected.

"I've had just about enough of this!" the other Oblique declared. Stepping over to one of the duplicate Time Yugos, he reached under the dash and tore out a handful of wires.

"Is anyone in there?" Doctor Prowse called out, rattling the doorknob.

6

"You mustn't damage the wiring in that duplicate Time Yugo!" the *fifth* Oblique declared, leaping out of the fifth Time Yugo almost before it finished shimmering into existence. The laboratory was becoming quite crowded.

"And why not?" demanded the other Oblique.

"You're doing irreparable damage to the timeline!" Oblique #5 told him.

"Your timeline or mine?" the other Oblique said dismissively.

"Your *place* or mine?" the other Emily said, winking at Emily #4 as she also climbed out of the fifth Time Yugo.

"Good one!" Emily #4 said, and the two Emilys high-fived. "Why is that us crying?" she asked, indicating the (previously) latest Emily.

"Her timeline's been invalidated, or something," the other Emily shrugged.

"Bummer."

The Obliques continued to argue until, inevitably, a scuffle broke out between two of them. The other three were all shouting over one another.

"This sucks," said the other Emily. "I just wanted to see Ancient Rome."

"We should just borrow one of the Yugos and check it out," Emily #4 said. "They don't even know we're here. They'll never miss us."

"We should take that us too though," the other Emily said, indicating the original. "I'd hate that me to miss out."

"She won't. If she's from our future she'll remember it, and if she's from our past she'll do exactly what we're about to do, only later."

"Good thinking!"

"What about *that* us?" Emily #4 asked, indicating the (formerly) latest Emily, who was bawling uncontrollably now.

"Forget her. She's obviously a pill."

The two of them climbed into the nearest Yugo, the

other Emily threw it into reverse, and they blinked out of existence.

7

With a boom of displaced air, the Time Yugo appeared in ancient Rome, right in the middle of a busy thoroughfare. Roman citizens gaped or fled or merely stared at it quizzically. The two Emilys climbed out.

"It's breathtaking!" the first Emily said. "Oh my gosh, look at the statues! They're not white like I've always pictured them! Honestly, they're kind of gaudy and tacky."

"I think we read somewhere that classical statuary was, in fact, quite colorful, and the paint just wore off over time."

"We did read that, didn't we?"

"So what do you want to see first?"

"A Roman orgy, obviously."

"We're so naughty! But seriously, there's no social media back now. Well, maybe Friendster. How do we locate the nearest orgy?"

The second Emily thought for a moment.

"Maaaayyybe... if we start, others will just join in."

"Well, okay. But remember – we have to be careful. If we change anything in the past, anything at all, even just stepping on a single butterfly, the Nazis will win World War II."

"Dur. I'm not stupid."

Just as Emily was about to take herself into her arms, a second Time Yugo appeared.

"Get in this car *immediately!*" a Professor Oblique demanded from the driver's seat. "You ladies have no

163

idea what you've done!"

8

The redundantly-labeled Time Chronometer (formerly the mileage indicator) read 2018, but they were surrounded by nonplussed, fully-uniformed Nazis!

"Oh no!" Professor Oblique groaned. "Now you've done it! Now you've really gone and done it!"

"This is a production of *The Diary of Anne Frank*," one of the Nazis said in perfect, unaccented English. "Would you kindly get your electric car off the stage?"

Oblique checked his spacial indicator.

"Oops, forgot to carry the two. Sorry."

The Yugo vanished.

9

A sixth Time Yugo appeared in the lab. A sixth professor Oblique occupied the driver's seat, and two Emilys were making out with each other in the back.

"Holy crap, I'm a lesbian?" one of the Emilys witnessing this exclaimed. "I'm so proud of myself!"

"Unless that counts as incest," another Emily countered.

"Or I'm just a total narcissist," a third Emily suggested.

Regardless, Ancient Rome had clearly been very educational.

"I found them," said this most recent Oblique, climbing out of the vehicle.

"Found who..." the Oblique who was speaking did a quick head count "...Number 6?"

164

"Why, our foolish assistants! They traveled all the way back to..." He looked around the room. By rights, they should be less one Time Yugo – now abandoned in ancient Rome – and a couple of Emilys. But this wasn't the case.

"Obviously you undershot your target time," said another Oblique, shaking his head. "You should have returned after you left, maintaining our number at five, not six. Instead, you've apparently returned *before*, muddling things still further."

"Well observed, Number 3," said yet another Oblique.

"I'm Number 1."

"No, *I'm* Number 1."

"Oh let's not start *that* again!"

"So wait," said the newly dubbed Number 6, "they haven't stolen the car yet?" He glared at each Emily in turn. "But you were just about to, right?" he demanded. They all shrugged. "Oh, I'm in a completely different timeline altogether!" he groaned, burying his face in his hands.

"Not necessarily," Number 1 said. "We've numbered ourselves based on what we think is an accurate 'outside the timeline' timeline of events, making you Number 6. I'm Number 1, and the others are, of course, Numbers 2 through 5. N1 through N6, for brevity. Our assistants have done the same."

"Except we picked cool names, like 'Emily Prime' and 'Atomic Sex Emily'," one of the Emilys interjected. Ignoring this, Oblique Number 1 stepped over to his whiteboard, marker in hand, and began outlining a plan of action.

"Now, we're in general agreement that N3 should be the first to *blah blah blah blah...*"

"This is *so* boring," said Duchess Unicorn Emily.

"I agree," said Emily Prime.

"You know," said Pumpkin Spice Emily, "there's a new bar on campus that actually has a liquor license."

"Well what are we waiting for?" Atomic Sex Emily asked. Redundantly, of course.

Collecting the two most recent Emilys, they slipped out the door. The Obliques never even noticed that they were gone.

10

"Twenty?" one of the six identical girls standing in front of him huffed. "If you add our ages up, we're *one hundred* and twenty!"

"It doesn't work that way," sighed the bartender. "You can't add different people's ages up."

"But we're *not* different people," countered Pumpkin Spice Emily. "We're the same person."

"Which is why we only charged you one cover charge. You can't have it both ways."

"Why not? Timeline overlap resulting in multiple iterations of a single entity is an entirely new concept. Who are you to apply arbitrary rules to this exciting new field?"

The bartender crossed his arms.

"Let's try a different approach," Duchess Unicorn Emily said. "These two mes..." she indicated the Emilys in question "...will make out for a full minute if you serve us."

"Hmmm..." the bartender said.

"To us!" Emily Prime said five minutes later, raising her pint. It was a true pint, not a niggardly American one. The other five Emilys toasted her.

"Do you think Professor Oblique will ever get this straightened out?" Ninja Emily asked.

"I suppose." Atomic Sex Emily frowned. "We'll know when some of us start disappearing. In a proper timeline, there can only be one Emily."

"The world will be a darker place," Gay Pride Emily lamented, staring into her beer.

"Well, there's nothing for it," Pumpkin Spice Emily said, putting on a brave face. She drained her pint. "Last one to blink out of existence picks up the tab!"

Their Own Little Corner of Heaven

Derek laid the last card down. "Won again," he said.

"Huh?" Scott looked up from his book.

"Solitaire," said his companion. "I won again."

"S'nice." Scott returned to his book, trying to find his place. Derek was laying out another game, seven cards across, the top card of each pile turned face-up. He began the play. Count out three cards, ah, I can play the six of hearts. Three more...

Fifteen minutes later the game was over. "Won again," he said.

"You always win," replied Scott, not bothering to look up this time. Derek thought about it for a moment. He **did** always win. How odd. He looked around the room as he shuffled the cards – white carpeting, white walls, furnished with a matching pair of white loveseats. Scott sat on one of these. The other was empty. There was a clear glass coffee table positioned between the loveseats, but Derek preferred playing on the floor. He felt more comfortable that way; more room to lay out the cards. The room was brightly, yet comfortably lit, though there were no visible sources of illumination, nor windows. There was a single door, but it was closed, and neither man had ever felt the urge to try and open it.

Derek began laying out another game. He heard Scott sigh. Suddenly a thought occurred to him.

"Scott?" he asked, "What page are you on?" Scott hesitated a moment before he answered.

"Fifty-nine."

Derek pondered this for a moment. "How many pages are in that book?" He watched Scott flip to the end, taking care to look at the page number and not the text above.

"Two hundred and four."

Derek began his play. Ace up top, red nine on the black ten... He continued thusly, until he won.

"I always win," he muttered.

"What?" asked Scott, not looking up. Derek didn't answer and his friend didn't ask again. Derek waited a while, then asked,

"Scott, what page are you on?" Scott checked.

"Fifty-nine."

Derek fiddled with his cards. "I asked you that a long time ago," he said.

"What?" asked Scott, finally looking up.

"A long time ago. I asked you what page you were on and you were on fifty-nine. You're always on fifty-nine."

"That was only a few minutes ago," replied Scott, dismissing him.

"No, no, I mean a **long** time ago. I'm sure of it. Fifty-nine. You're always on fifty-nine."

Scott was ignoring him. Derek had, almost unconsciously, laid out another game. He looked at the cards in disgust.

"I'm going to win," he said. He reshuffled the deck and dealt it out again, Vegas style. Much more difficult odds. He played and won. He gathered up the cards and shuffled them idly. He wondered how much time had passed – he wished there were a clock in the room.

"I'm going to open the door," he declared.

"Why?" asked Scott, clearly disinterested.

"Are you on page fifty-nine?"

"Uh-huh...." Scott finally closed his book, saving his place with his thumb. "What's wrong?" he asked.

"I dunno, I... I always win. I dunno..." Derek trailed off.

"People like to win," Scott reminded him. "Aren't you content?" Derek stared at the cards.

"I guess so."

"Okay, then." Scott opened his favorite book back to page fifty-nine. Derek laid out the cards again. He played a game and won. If he weren't so content he would scream and scream and scream and scream...

Uncle Amjad's Email

Charlie! Good to hear from you! I'm sorry we haven't had a chance to talk since the funeral, and I'm sorry to hear about your recent troubles at school. I miss my brother very much, and your mother, who really was the sister I never had. Not a day goes by that I don't think of them, and I can understand how difficult it must be for you to concentrate on your studies when the degree you're pursuing was as much their dream as it is yours. If your grades continue to slip, perhaps you could withdraw from your classes and take a semester off? Better to be a bit behind than to torpedo your GPA.

On to your primary concern. You asked me, in no uncertain terms, if I think your parents are "out there somewhere" and are "watching over you" and that's a question no one can answer, of course. But let me tell you a little story, a true story, and maybe that will help.

When I was 29 I got my first real job at the firm in L.A. , the one I worked at until I transferred in 2009. This was in the summer of 2001, and as you can no doubt imagine the tail end of 2001 was a bad time to be Muslim in the United States of America. I was already going through a pretty rough time. My girlfriend (we were pre-engaged at the time, whatever that even means) had left me, money was tight, I, truthfully, wasn't particularly good at my new job, and then the world went crazy and suddenly everyone seemed to be giving me sideways glances and treating me like a pariah. I know I'm not the only one who went through this, and many got it far worse than I, but on top of everything else it felt like the world was closing in around me, crushing me. I couldn't breathe, couldn't think, sleepwalked through every day and kept sinking deeper and deeper into depression as my work performance suffered and it looked more and more like I would lose my job, any day, any second. Perhaps if I had had some sort of support group, but I knew no one in L.A. and my father (that would be your great uncle, you never met him) was far from supportive of my career choice. He had essentially disowned me at this point (he relented somewhat, later) and even forbade my mother to speak to me. So I was alone, in a strange city, frightened, drowning. Most days I spent in a haze, wishing I were a child again. I even had dreams in which I WAS a child again, safe and secure in the knowledge that my parents had all the answers and would take care of everything. I suppose that's what started me thinking about the Friend Ship. Now you probably don't know this program because it was well before your time, although I believe they still run it on PBS from time to time, and for all I know it's on your Netflix. It was a children's show during the 1970s and well into the 80s although I suspect it was just reruns by the end. The show took place on a boat, the Friend Ship. Captain Horatio Montgomery Stump, all 6'4" of him, was in charge. The rest of the crew, silly characters with names like "First Mate Worstmate" and such, were puppets, although I believe the Captain provided all their voices. Hokey stuff. It was your typical educational program, but it wasn't all flashy and hyperactive with songs and perpetual motion and that sort of exhausting energy. And it didn't teach numbers or letters or American history or anything like that. It was a gentle show. Captain HMS (you see the play on words, I assume) was silly and slapsticky, but always kind. His jokes were never demeaning or at the expense of another person. And he always addressed the audience, the children at home, directly, as his friends, talking to us like we were right there, aboard the ship with him. He spoke to children like they were adults, and discussed things like divorce and being scared and all the things kids worry about but don't always share with their parents. And he was never judgemental. My father, quite frankly, didn't like me watching the show. He said it would make me a "sissy" and "queer". I didn't know what that meant so I looked it up in the dictionary, which only said that it meant "weird" or "unusual". When I asked my father to explain he said "I meant gay." So I looked THAT up and the dictionary said it meant 'happy'. Needless to say, I was almost a teenager before I figured out what he was really saying. By then, of course, it was "hip" amongst the more cynical of us to make fun of the show, implying that Captain HMS was probably a pedophile and such. Immature garbage talk, bashing something we'd loved, but outgrown.

But in that miserable fall of 2001 I thought about the Friend Ship a lot. Maybe I even thought about it that last day, although I don't remember. See, I'd decided to kill myself. I had a whole, wild plan cooked up too. I was afraid to use a gun, wasn't quite sure where to get one anyhow, so I'd procured some pills and planned to do it that way. I'd also purchased a CD containing the theme from those Charlie Brown specials they always used to show on TV. (Do they still run those, during the holidays? You know the ones I mean, I hope.) My plan, childishly dramatic, was to play this CD, full blast, and put it on repeat after I swallowed the pills. I guessed that I would certainly be dead by the time enough of the neighbours in my apartment building complained and summoned other people who summoned the authorities who finally broke down the door. They would burst in and there I'd be, stone dead, while the happiest music imaginable played over and over as my ghoulish eulogy. Yes, I thought I was so wickedly clever. I might have even been smiling, for the first time in months, as I left work that day, secure in my vengeance. In a few hours I would be dead. That would show them.

Now, our firm handled a few celebrity clients, mostly what you'd call "D-listers" I guess (although we did briefly handle one A-lister at the time, the comedian Robin Williams). So it wasn't unusual to see a minor celebrity or two roaming around the building. But that night, when I passed one of these "minor celebrities" as I was leaving, I froze in my tracks. He was wearing a three-piece suit and carrying a briefcase, and he was several years older, but his face, his build, the man was unmistakeable. It was Captain Horatio Montgomery Stump, in the flesh! I said something out loud, "Wow" or "Oh my god" or maybe even an expletive, I don't remember. He probably got that sort of thing all the time, but instead of simply giving me a nod or a polite smile as he passed he stopped too and favoured me with the biggest smile you've ever seen. "My friend!" he said, just like that, like we'd known each other for years. "How are you?" "I served on your crew," I said, smiling. "Of course you did!" he said, like it was the most natural thing in the world. "I'm bad with names but I remember your face!" And I just started to cry, right there, in front of him and the cleaning crew and a few office stragglers. "What's wrong?" he asked me, just as genuine as can be, and suddenly I was sobbing, sobbing, great heaving sobs that made my chest ache. "I don't know what to do I don't know what to do!" I just kept saying over and over and I felt like a damned fool but I didn't care.

So he walked me over to a bench in the adjoining lobby and sat me down and I was about to thank him when, to my total surprise, he sat down next to me and set his briefcase aside. "Tell me about it," he said. So I did. I told him about my breakup and my job and how I didn't have any friends and how the whole world seemed to hate me and 9/11 and everything, and he listened and he nodded but he wasn't just listening and nodding he was LISTENING. And when I was done he nodded again and he told me that, when his show ended (sometime in the 1980s, I guess?) he was out of work for quite some time. See, he wasn't just an actor, he had degrees and wrote books, he was a kind of expert on child psychology. But everyone knew him for the show, so when they stopped producing new episodes his books went out of print and the speaking engagements dried up and eventually he was broke. Finally, he told me, he was evicted from his house and, that night, he found himself sleeping on the beach. There he was, Captain Horatio Montgomery Stump, master of the seven-and-a-half seas (that was one of the show's little jokes; the "half sea" was his bathtub, IIRC), sleeping on a beach. You had to laugh. "When I woke up on that beach the next morning," he told me, "I said to myself 'What can I do, today, to make this situation just a little bit better?'" And that's all you can do, he told me. Just use each day to make the situation a little better. And, pretty soon, things will be a lot better. Because we've all been there. Even the people you think are the bravest and the strongest and the smartest have been there.

I thanked him and we stood up and I said I was sorry if I made him late for a meeting or something and he just smiled at me like that was just the silliest thing in the world to say. "That's what friends are for," he said. And he meant it. Then he scooped up his briefcase and ran for the elevator and just made it and waved to me as the doors closed. I waved back and then I went home and poured those pills down the drain and got to work making it better, one day at a time. And finally, one day, it WAS better.

I've told this story dozens of times since to friends and clients, but I always have to fudge the details a little bit. See, this occurred in late November or possibly early December of 2001, I know because of the whole 9/11 thing. What I didn't know then is that Captain Horatio Montgomery Stump, real name Henry Jacob Marshall, had died of pancreatic cancer in 1998.

I hope this helps in some small way.

Peace and Blessings upon you

your Uncle Amjad

Phonomania

Everyone is just standing here
Waiting for uniforms;
Waiting to sell their youth,
Waiting to die conform...

1

I took off the headphones.

"Well, what do you think?" Antoine asked.

"It's okay, I guess," I said. "What's 'die conform'?"

"I dunno. I think they just needed an extra syllable in there." He lit a cigarette. He liked to smoke inside, not because he enjoyed it, but because it bothered people. "How would you categorize it?" he asked.

"Hmm. Melancholy, but hooky. A little too synthy. Overproduced, but that's 1986 for you. Post-punk, I guess? A friend of mine in college called this style 'the stuff that punk rockers' girlfriends always seem to listen to'."

"Our crowd called it 'limp-wrister rock'." He shrugged. "It was a less enlightened era."

"And you and your crowd were probably fist-pumping it to Judas Priest at the time," I pointed out.

"We were," he admitted, snubbing out his cigarette. He'd only smoked a quarter of it.

"So what's supposed to happen, exactly?" I asked. He shrugged again.

"Wait," he said.

"It's all just a little hard to swallow, like your

coffee." I grimaced as I took another sip. It tasted like it had been filtered through a dirty sock. Then, just like that, it got away from me and I spilled the remainder of the cup down the front of my shirt. "Shit!" I looked up at Antoine. "Was that it?"

"Could be," he said. "Probably. But there's no way of knowing for sure."

"Power of suggestion," I suggested. I smiled at my little joke. "What's supposed to happen if I listen to it again?"

"Escalation. The coffee will be scalding hot next time. Or you'll fall down the stairs. Your dog will get hit by a car. Could be anything."

"And it gets worse each time?"

"So they say."

"I'm not buying it." Antoine's face fell. "The story, I mean. I'm still buying the vinyl."

"Oh, I'm not selling the original. Just a burn."

"I happen to have a thumb drive right here with me," I said, reaching into my pocket. Antoine shook his head.

"Sorry. I'm gonna ask you not to share copies with anyone, or sell them, but I know you will, so at the very least I'm going to make you go through the trouble of ripping it off the disc."

"Okay," I said. "How much?"

"Seven grand, and I'll throw in the rest of the album as a bonus. Nine additional songs."

"Don't need 'em," I said. "I'll write you a check."

"What is this, the 1950s?" he scoffed, pulling out his phone. "I've got Square."

"Mind if I spin my copy before I leave, make sure it's okay?"

"Be my guest, just use the headphones."

So I listened to "Waiting for Uniforms" for the second time that day. On the way home I got into a fender bender.

2

As a rule, musical curses are generally attached to artists. Every music fan is familiar with the 27 Club, referring to the inordinate number of famous musicians who died at that age. Robert Johnson, Brian Jones, Jimi Hendrix, Janis Joplin, Jim Morrison, Pete Ham, Chris Bell, Kurt Cobain, and Amy Winehouse are all members of that exclusive set. Classical composers, meanwhile, seem to die with alarming regularity after completing a ninth symphony. Then there's the curse reputedly attached to Buddy Holly and everyone who has been even peripherally connected to him, which is so convoluted by now that it probably includes his barber and the kid who stole his lunch money in the fifth grade. The bands Led Zeppelin and Bone Thugs-n-Harmony were reputedly cursed too.

There are specific songs that are said to be unlucky, though. Robert Johnson's "Crossroads", for example, is thought to heap misfortune on anyone who records it, and other songs rumored to be dangerous to play include "Stairway to Heaven" and "Sympathy for the Devil".

None of these "curses" are believed to effect the actual *listener*, however.

With two exceptions.

The first, and most famous, is "Gloomy Sunday", a Hungarian ballad written by a cat named Rezső Seress and most famously recorded by Billie Holiday

181

in 1941. It was (tenuously) connected to so many suicides that the BBC fucking banned it from airplay, a ban that wasn't lifted until *2002*. Seress himself committed suicide in the late 1960s, adding a nice, eerie coda to the whole thing.

The second is "Waiting for Uniforms", by a deliriously obscure 1980s band called No Diving. Their first, and only, LP, *Orange, Purple, Silver*, was initially notable only for its low press run (the actual number supposedly printed diminishes with each telling; I once heard a guy claim that only 200 promo copies were actually produced) and faux-clever, impenetrable song titles like "Crown on Town" and "I Smashed My Radio to Prove I Was the High Earl of Funk". There's no confirmed record of them ever playing live, they had no following, and only one of them, the bassist, went on to anything else, fronting an equally obscure spoken word/techno/overdub mash-up called Dirk Speedwell and the Explained, which released a single self-produced cassette single in or around 1989. Speedwell died in 1992 when the studio where he was recording material for a follow-up single, "Catholic Eater", mysteriously burned to the ground. Speedwell had repeatedly stated that the idea for "Catholic Eater", a 45-minute opus, came to him in a dream, but in the days leading up to his death he reportedly told several friends that he had come to believe that this dream came from the Devil, and that "Catholic Eater" was going to kill him.

The other members of No Diving didn't fare much better. The lead singer was decapitated in a motorcycle accident shortly after the release of *Orange, Purple, Silver*. The drummer committed suicide in 1989 in the wake of his wife's suicide, prompted by a miscarriage. It was the lead guitarist who would suffer the most ignominious, bizarre fate of all though, buried alive when a truck delivering several tons of fresh fish toppled over and burst in a Boston street. He was smothered to death before onlookers could dig him out.

So yeah, not the luckiest band in the world. We're talking Exploding Hearts levels of bad luck here. But at least the Exploding Hearts were talented. No Diving didn't even have that going for them. Not that they were irredeemably terrible, mind you, but they definitely hovered somewhere south of mediocre. Just another also-ran, unmemorable rock band.

But then something happened.

One of their songs, "Waiting for Uniforms" began to garner a bit of an... odd reputation.

Supposedly, it was unlucky.

Not unlucky for the band (that was a given), but unlucky to anyone unfortunate enough to hear even a snippet of it. The legend took a while to build – years, actually – in no small part because almost nobody ever listened to *Orange, Purple, Silver* on anything close to a regular basis. It just wasn't that good or memorable. But every band is somebody's favorite, or at least on their radar, and eventually people began to notice that bad things seemed to happen to them whenever they spun this platter.

3

The story initially circulated solely amongst that subset of record collectors who are enamored with post-punk or proto-goth or whatever the hell niche you care to cram No Diving into. Listening to

"Waiting for Uniforms" invited bad luck. And it was cumulative. Listen to it once, you might stub your toe. Listen to it a score of times, and you were courting disaster. The immediate results were never really dramatic enough for the story to filter into the mainstream though, like, say, the story of Bloody Mary or that bullshit about Coca-Cola dissolving a penny. Someone would pick up on the legend, get their hands on the album, spin it once or twice, and, when nothing overtly dramatic happened, forget about it. Oh they might miss their favorite TV show that night, or their plumbing would back up, but they'd rarely make the connection. Even if they did, almost no one pushed it, to see how far it would go.

Almost no one.

In October of 2003 a guy (of course it was a guy) named Ricky Henderson (no, not the baseball player) decided to write an article for the local liberal/music rag about the urban legend surrounding "Waiting for Uniforms". He obtained a copy and listened to the song first thing in the morning, every day, for a month, keeping a journal in which he noted, in minute detail, every niggling mishap and inconvenience that befell him, with plans to compare and contrast these notes with a similar journal he kept the month before, prior to listening to the song. His notes are filled with an escalating series of misfortunes – unsubstantiated, of course – from money lost in vending machines to computer crashes to flat tires. On Day 9 we're told that his girlfriend unexpectedly broke up with him. Day 10 contains the journal's most cryptic entry though:

10-10 More of the same. Got chewed out by the

boss (again) because of those missing invoices. Says I'm skating on thin ice. Blew my engine on the way home (this is getting expensive!) Had to walk the rest of the way home & of course it started raining. Hail, even, for about 60 seconds. Weird homeless-looking guy followed me for about 3 blocks. Figured he was gonna mug me but we reached my place & I got inside before he got his nerve up, I guess. Way things are going, he'll get me tomorrow. Here's some weirdness: Guy in a dark suit came to my work today & told me I need to back off this thing. Says it's not what I think. Wondering how he even knew about it, since no one knows except me & Eddie & Keith. Probably just a nut but I'm meeting him tonight. Can't hurt to add an extra layer of crazy to this article.

Ricky Henderson died that night, October 10/11, when he jumped or fell from the roof of a parking garage near his apartment building. It was ultimately deemed a suicide, prompted by the recent breakup with his long-time girlfriend. His journal ended up on eBay, which is where I got it. His copy of the No Diving album mysteriously vanished.

Oh yeah, about that. Copies of this album have a way of disappearing. Like, one day you'll go to pull it out and it just won't be there any more. Or someone will burgle your pad and steal the TV, stereo, laptop, jewelry... and just this one obscure record album. You'd think the advent of the Internet would make it easier than ever to find a copy, for those who wanted to, but the opposite seems to be true. When copies do turn up the asking price is outrageous, above and beyond even the fancies of the most deluded Amazon seller. Hell, I've seen the *empty sleeve* go for fifty bucks on auction sites. If you do find a copy online, pay the extra for the postal insurance. They have a habit of getting irreparably damaged during shipping.

Long story otherwise, it's not the easiest record to come by these days.

So when Antoine casually mentioned that he'd stumbled onto a copy, part of a huge, unsorted collection he had recently purchased, I was ecstatic. But I played it cool. Pretended I'd never heard of it. The key to dealing with sellers – with people, really – is to always let them think that they've got the upper hand.

4

Okay, so you might have noticed that I'm a little obsessed with this song, and I am, but not for the reasons you'd think. Oh, I'm a collector; it's how I learned about "Waiting for Uniforms" in the first place. But I don't collect 1980s shit. To me, most '80s music sounds like the incidental pop/rock tunes you'd hear in a Hollywood movie, the ones that aren't even worth putting on the soundtrack. Soulless crap. I have a much more... practical... interest in owning a copy of "Waiting for Uniforms".

Let me tell you about my wife.

We'll skip all the boring stuff, like how we met and how big her tits are (pretty big), and get right to the meat of it.

She's a goddamned cunt.

She's a goddamned cunt and I hate her fucking guts.

She's also stupefyingly bad at a great deal of

186

things. Like cooking. And not fucking the pool boy. And technology.

That last one is key. See, she just has to have all the latest gewgaws, but she doesn't know how to use any of them. She can't even check her email without my help, never mind navigating the unintuitive intricacies of your average smart phone.

So I'm going to make "Waiting for Uniforms" her ring tone.

I'm out of town on business for the next week, so hopefully that will be enough time. It should be; bitch is always on the phone, even when she's driving. I'm surprised she hasn't rear-ended somebody and killed *herself* long before now. So a week ought to do it. I'll call her a few times myself, just to make sure. And if it works, if it really works...

Email attachments.

File sharing.

Streaming video.

Online radio?

I'll have to change the file name though. After all, a lot more people are likely to open "Pictures from grandma" or "New Taylor Swift album", right? And the mark only needs to hear it for an instant. Hell, I could just dub a couple of seconds over an otherwise legitimate video. Who knows, maybe something I append it to will even go viral. Might want to invest in some earplugs, ha ha!

My God, but we're going to have a time.

Booyah.

The Little White Duck

ONCE UPON A TIME there was a little white duck who was very sad. He was sad because he could not get pectoral implants. Because of this, the little duck thought that he was a wimp.

One day, the little duck was walking by the pond with his friend, Mr. Bullfrog. Mr. Bullfrog wasn't really a bullfrog, he was just a regular old frog frog. But they called him "Mr. Bullfrog" because he was full of it, if you catch our drift.

Anyway, Mr. Bullfrog was saying "I remember back in '76 when I was out cruisin' with the Sex Pistols and we were all blasted on coke and they wanted to introduce me to the lead singer of some band they knew, 'cause she was a frog, too, ya see..."

"That never happened," said the little duck. "You were only born this spring. How could you have done anything in 1976?" Mr. Bullfrog got angry.

"Are you calling me a liar?" he croaked, "Why, I oughta kick your butt, you wimp − but you're not even worth the trouble!"

As soon as Mr. Bullfrog called the little duck a wimp, he (the duck) began to cry.

"Wak-wak boo-hoo," he cried.
"Wak-wak boo-hoo
Sob wak-wak
Wak-wak-wak-wak."

Mr. Bullfrog found this particularly annoying, so he hopped home to watch something on the Fox network.

After a time, the little duck stopped crying, but he still felt sad. So he went to see his friend, The Ant. While "The Ant" sounds like he might be a bookie, or maybe some sort of rap musician, he was really just that – an ant. (The) Ant lived by himself because he was a little red ant, and the rest of the red ants had died when the other ants gave them blankets infected with smallpox.

Ant was the little duck's best friend. Ant used to have another friend, Grasshopper, but they had had a falling-out. Ant used to work and work, while Grasshopper sang and danced. This went on for many months. One day Ant said, "When winter comes, you will be sorry you played and didn't work, Grasshopper!" And Grasshopper said,

"This is southern Florida, winter never comes."

So Ant killed and ate him.

When the little duck got to Ant's house, Ant was reading an old copy of *Fate* magazine and drinking his favorite mixed drink, a grasshopper. "Bitter irony!" he would laugh. "Ha ha! Ha ha ha ha ha ha ha ha ha ha HA!"

Sometimes the little duck worried about Ant.

When Ant saw his friend he began to wave. "Duck!" he yelled, "Duck!"

Suddenly a golf ball hit the little duck in the head. "I told you to duck," sighed Ant.

"I don't care if I get hit by a million golf balls," said the little duck. "I don't even care if I get hit by a million million golf balls."

"That's a lot of balls," agreed Ant. "What is making you so sad?" he asked his friend as they hid in the high grass from the irate golfer whose ball had hit the little duck and then rolled into the pond.

"Shit!" said the golfer. "Dammit!"

"I'm sad because Mr. Bullfrog called me a wimp," the little duck told Ant. "If only I had pectoral implants! Then I could beat him to a pulp and say something clever."

"Like 'I toad-ally kicked your ass'?" asked Ant.

"Exactly."

Ant thought and thought, but he could not figure out what the little duck could do about his problem. Finally he said, "Perhaps you should ask the owls. They are the wisest of all the animals that live around the pond." Actually, Ant knew that the owls were a pair of cantankerous, senile pains-in-the-ass, but he was getting bored with the little duck and wanted to get back to his drink. To Ant's relief, the little duck said,

"That is a grand idea! Thank you, Ant!"And off he waddled in the direction of the old owls' tree on the other side of the pond.

What a jackass, thought Ant.

The little duck walked for a long time, all the way around the pond. He could fly, of course, just like any other duck, but in addition to being weak the little duck was a tad dim.

When he reached the big old tree on the far shore he saw the two old owls asleep on a branch. He was filled with awe and fear.

"Look at those hooters," he said. "I'm just a little duck, they will never help me." But the little duck was determined to try, because it was certainly easier than fighting his own battles.

"Wise owls!" he cried. "Oh, wise owls! Please help me!" The owls looked down at the little duck, hoping that whomever had woken them up would be small enough to eat. But the little duck was too big.

"What is it?" sighed one of the owls. He was tired of all the animals who lived near the pond always coming around and bothering them.

"Mr. Bullfrog calls me a wimp and I can't pummel him and then say something clever because I don't have pectoral implants!"

"Something like 'You won't frog-get that beating'?" asked the owl.

"Exactly."

"Perhaps you are a wimp," said the other owl, "or you wouldn't need pectoral implants."

And this made the little duck cry again.

"Wak-wak boo-hoo," he cried.
"Wak-wak boo-hoo,
Sob wak-wak
Wak-wak-wak-wak."

This went on for some time.
"God, that's annoying," said the first owl.
"Think of something so he'll go away," said the

second.

So the first owl said to the little duck: "I know who can help you, little duck. The pike who lives in the pond owes us a favor. If you remove yourself to the very center of the pond and call out 'Pikey, pikey, likey, likey' he will swim to the surface. Just tell him you are our friend, and he will help you." Actually, the pike would come to the surface if you simply called out his name, but the owl thought it would be funnier if the little duck made a fool out of himself.

"Thank you! Oh, thank you!" said the little duck.

"Go away," said the owls.

The little duck waddled into the pond and began to swim. He swam and swam. He could have flown but, well, you know. Finally he was at the very center. He took a deep breath and shouted,

"Pikey, pikey,
Likey likey!"

Deep down in the water, the pike heard the little duck. "What the hell is he doing?" the pike wondered. So he swam up to see.

"What is going on, duck?" he asked the little duck. "Why are you yelling?"

"The owls said you could help me," said the little duck. "Mr. Bullfrog has been teasing me and I want him to stop."

"Mr. Bullfrog?" asked the pike. "The one who's in the Senate?"

"Grrrr..." said the little duck.

The pike thought and thought. Finally he said "Since you are a friend of the owls, I will help you. But they'd better delete those pictures now!"

So the pike swam around and around the pond until he found Mr. Bullfrog, who was telling the other frogs about his days at Harvard. And the pike swam right up to him and gobbled him up.

"Yum," said the pike, who decided he would have to eat frogs more often, much to their dismay.

"Hooray!" said the little duck. He was very happy. And best of all, he had learned how satisfying revenge could be. He decided that he would make many more enemies, preferably smaller than himself.

He would start with Ant.

THE END

Parking Lot World

He wondered, not for the first time, if the sun were worse than the rain. There was no shelter from either, but at least the rain served a purpose. One needed water. Of course, sometimes the sun provided a most welcome warmth, when the air was chill and damp, but all too often it simply cooked you alive, baking you in your own skin.

He paused, his eyes tracing the faded white lines just visible on the broken asphalt. The same pattern, of course, always the same pattern. One long one with several parallel lines sprouting out from it, evenly spaced to create two rows of perfect rectangles, each open at one end. As a child he'd been taught that they had some religious significance, but he couldn't remember the details, and it hardly mattered to him now.

He was a confirmed atheist. He didn't believe in Store.

There was an island ahead, a small one. One tenacious slick-bush, it's leaves waxy and black-green. Tall, yellowed grass. That meant no water. But there was a light tree nearby, and already it was flickering to life as the sun dipped below the horizon. A soft place to sleep, and light. There were worse places to spend the night. Matting down the grass, he made a little nest for himself. He clutched the pack containing his meager belongings tightly to his breast as he settled in, making it impossible to lift without waking him. Satisfied, he closed his eyes. Oblivion claimed him almost immediately.

Someone was coming. He heard it in his sleep, soles smacking the asphalt. Directionless, purposeless. He could tell by the sound of their footfalls. Slowly sitting up he watched as a youth made for the island. Made for him. The youth spotted him and hesitated. He didn't peg the youth as a lifter, though. A lifter wouldn't have made so much noise. He raised a single hand in greeting. The youth, who had clearly been walking for some time, closed the distance between them and plopped down on the asphalt. He carried no personal belongings.

"Where do you come from?" he asked the youth. The youth stared at him blankly.

So he didn't speak Guest. Not surprising.

"Nathan," he said, tapping his own chest. Then he pointed at the youth.

"Torc," the boy said, indicating himself. His eyes were full of questions.

"Here," Nathan said, fishing a plastic bottle out of his pack. It was badwater, but it was better than nothing. Torc drank from the bottle greedily. He was clearly from Somewhere Else; Nathan had crossed paths with his kind before. Frightened and confused, he wouldn't last long. Nathan felt a twinge of pity for the boy though, and, feeling companionable, did not object when Torc assumed to join him.

The great asphalt sea stretched to the horizon in every direction. It had always been so. His new companion seemed fascinated by this, constantly craning his neck as if he expected to discover something on the horizon, as if there were some destination, some point. Just past noon Nathan extracted the sling from his pack and brought down a greybird for lunch. He ate it raw, feathers and all, taking time to discard only the beak and bones. Torc refused to partake. Maybe in his world fire was ubiquitous, but here fuel was scarce, cooked meat a luxury. He would learn. They passed no few islands, most of little interest, but one was adorned with flowers, pink and robust, and this caught Nathan's attention. Sure enough, a water nodule was hidden amongst the blossoms, so they waited until it triggered and Nathan refilled the plastic water bottle Torc had drained, and two more besides. Badwater, but it was better than no water, and one never knew, for certain, when the rain might come again. Nathan scoffed at the little yellow sign planted next to the nodule: "Do Not Drink".

About a hour later Torc grew excited at the appearance of some signage. He seemed to read great significance into its appearance, and Nathan strove to convey to him that it was simply a religious marker.

They'd come upon a road – designated by low, regularly-spaced bumps – that wound through an unusually dense grouping of islands. Religious markers were common in places like this, urging people to STOP sinning, to YIELD to Store. Torc made it clear that he wanted to explore, and, seeing no harm in this, Nathan permitted it. They drifted from one island to the next, Torc growing increasingly frustrated when they found nothing of any interest. There was shade, however, from several greentrees that sprouted from the larger islands, and multiple water nodules, so they lingered for a time, rested, drank their fill. Torc balked at drinking the badwater from its source, but took some more from one of Nathan's bottles, apparently unaware that it was the same water. Nathan did nothing to enlighten him.

Finally they moved on.

Just past three-quarter-day, there was trouble. Cart Boys, driving a caravan of forty carts or more, lashed together five wide and at least eight deep. Their leaders, the Seniority, rode, while the rest pushed. The carts in the center of the caravan were laden with all manner of goods, and these Boys were intent on adding to their cache, so when they spotted Nathan and Torc several runners broke from the group and gave chase. One – a girl – would not give up, and when she unwittingly outdistanced her confederates to such a degree that they were lost to sight Nathan suddenly reversed direction and ran full-bore into her, putting his shoulder into her chest and completely bowling her over. She landed on her rump.

"Ow!" she cried out. She looked over her shoulder, expecting help, only then realizing that the others had long since given up the chase. She turned her hate-filled eyes on Nathan. "I'll bite it off!" she hissed through the brown-blonde hair that fell across her face.

"Do not flatter yourself," Nathan sneered. He gave her the once-over, favored her with an additional sneer, then turned and strode away. Torc hesitantly followed.

"Have a nice day!" the girl shouted after them. *"Have a nice day!"* This was understood to be an epithet, roughly the equivalent of "Fuck you!"

Torc kept looking back.

"She's pretty, yes, but not to be trusted." Nathan knew the lad couldn't understand him. Probably he was trying to convince himself.

"I'll die out here!" the girl wailed. "Please don't leave me!"

"Go back to your tribe!" Nathan shouted.

"I'll *die*," the girl sobbed.

Torc had stopped walking.

Nathan sighed. Curse fate and its mischievous whims. Now he had an entourage.

"Thank you for coming back for me," Jenyver smiled. Too cute, far too young, all baby fat and pug nose, her powder blue dress shirt rode up as she stretched, exposing her navel. Torc stared.

"My young friend's eyes are going to pop out of his head," Nathan said.

"Why doesn't he talk?" Jenyver asked. She sat down on the curb delineating the tiny island where Nathan had decided they would spend the night.

"He does, but I can't understand him. He doesn't speak Guest."

"Then he's from Somewhere Else?"

"He wouldn't be the first."

"Maybe he was sent by Store."

"If you believe in that sort of thing." He was in no mood for a metaphysical discussion.

"I believe there *is* a Store, and some day we'll be delivered."

"Why didn't you go back to your people?" Nathan asked, eager to change the subject. Jenyver looked away.

"It's not easy being the only cart *girl* in a tribe of Cart Boys," she said quietly.

"I see." Nathan smirked.

"It's not funny!"

"No?"

"Can I help you to your car?" she snapped.

"There's no need to be crass," he said.

They walked for days with no set goal in mind. Nomads navigating a plain of cracked asphalt. Torc learned to eat greybird, uncooked. They stumbled across an abandoned cart, but one of the wheels was missing and they ultimately abandoned it. One day it rained, and they huddled together miserably because there was no shelter in sight. Still, this provided them with several bottles of rainwater, always preferable to badwater. Torc learned a few words of Guest, but nowhere near enough to ask the questions that danced in his eyes, or understand the answers, even if Nathan had any.

A week after the girl joined them, it happened.

"Look! Oh, look!" she shouted. She had scampered ahead of them that day, overflowing with a sudden influx of youthful energy. She was staring at the asphalt.

"What?" asked Nathan.

"Blue!" she shouted back. "Blue lines!"

Nathan scoffed. Impossible. Superstitious twaddle.

But the girl was right. The open-ended, parallel rectangles scarring the asphalt *were* blue. Not white, not even yellow. Blue.

And at the center of each, white on a blue field, the symbol. A crooked line with a dot at one end, seated awkwardly in a half-circle. A religious symbol, it indicated enlightenment. A literal and spiritual proximity to... Store. Nathan shook his head. His hands were shaking too, he realized.

"No," he said. "No. It isn't possible."

"Maybe we died," Jenyver whispered reverently, and the idea hit Nathan like a punch to the gut. He replayed the events of the last several hours in his mind. Nothing unusual had happened. There was no dramatic *point* where they might have unknowingly... died... and slipped from this world into the next.

The asphalt still felt as solid as ever beneath his feet.

He could still feel the sun, the breeze.

Torc looked at him questioningly.

"We should turn around," Nathan said quietly.

"No!" Jenyver said. "Don't you want to see? Don't you want to know?"

He didn't, he realized. But how could one not?

"Okay, then," he said.

Row after row after row of blue lines behind them, they finally saw it. A great, glittering edifice, rising from the asphalt, half again taller than the tallest light tree that Nathan had ever seen. Torc grew increasingly excited. Jenyver began quietly praying.

Nathan, already untethered, tumbled into a sort of silent awe.

There really is a Store, he thought. He had to blink back his tears, so as not to weep in front of the youngsters.

Closer, closer, looming over them now. They stepped over a curb and found themselves on an unbroken expanse of raised white asphalt, only not asphalt, because it was denser, smoother. All around them were things that Nathan had heard of, but had never believed truly existed. There was a Trash, a round receptacle where one was said to deposit things one no longer wanted, as if a person could afford to cavalierly discard any potentially useful item. Clearly, Store's kingdom was a kingdom of plenty. And there were Benches, several of them, where the chosen could loll about forever in decadent repose. Jenyver sprawled out across one of these, her shirt riding up to expose her navel again.

"It's *glorious*," she beamed.

Before them, a portal.

Nathan stepped forward. Through a pane of tinted glass he could see into the land beyond. Was it really the afterlife? Did it matter? There were wonders within.

He put his hand on the pull-bar that opened the portal. It beckoned him, the word PULL literally burned into it.

"Wait!" Jenyver cried.

Nathan looked to her questioningly.

"We can't go in like this," she said. She was already stripping of her powder blue shirt, her khakis. Torc gaped as she tossed even her undergarments aside. Nathan didn't stop her when she dug into his pack and extracted a bottle of water.

"Cleanse yourselves," she admonished, wetting her shirt and using it to wipe the grit from her hands and face. Nathan dropped his pack, removed his clothing, and followed suit.

Torc stared at them like they'd lost their minds. He backed away to disassociate himself, looking around furtively as if afraid someone were going to suddenly appear and chastise them.

"Torc..." Nathan said, beckoning him.

"No, he doesn't understand." Jenyver took Nathan's hand and their fingers automatically entwined. "He's from Somewhere Else. Maybe his purpose was to guide us here. Or maybe he's just not ready to enter Store's kingdom."

Nathan hesitated, but the girl, fresh and naked and smiling, was irresistibly convincing. Torc could follow if he so chose. He, Nathan, was not the boy's keeper.

"Now," Jenyver said, squeezing Nathan's hand.

Nathan gripped the pull-bar with his free hand and

tugged.

It held fast.

He pulled again and again, increasingly frustrated.

Still, nothing.

Then his eyes found the small, rectangular sign pasted on the far side of the glass.

He fell to his knees and despaired.

CLOSED, it said.

Christmas Memories

"Mein Gott!"

Josef stopped dead in his tracks, losing his granddaughter and her husband in the flood of last-minute holiday shoppers almost immediately. No, it was impossible. Yet...

A heavyset woman struggling with several packages had stepped into his line of sight, and he rudely pushed her aside, ignoring her indignant *"Well!"* as he scanned the crowd for the man he couldn't possibly have seen. It was Christmas Eve, 2004, and the man would be, what, a hundred years old by now? Not an absolute impossibility, of course, but...

No, it had to be his imagination. He was tired, it had been a long day, a long week. Hell, a long life. He was a tired, foolish old man, and he was seeing things. But no, there he was again! The man he couldn't possibly have seen, but did, was slowly, purposelessly navigating the crowd, his eyes downcast as if he were searching for lost change or a salvageable cigarette. Josef couldn't believe it, but there was no mistaking him, not even after all this time.

Josef strode quickly after him, his granddaughter, her husband, and their panicky, zero-hour shopping trip utterly forgotten.

The man seemed to be making his way slowly towards a side exit, and Josef lost him in the crowd more than once, doubting his certainly each time until he saw the man's face again, that face that he would never forget. The man had reached the short, nondescript hallway leading to the parking lot, where he suddenly paused, hesitating at the door as Josef caught up with him. He could have reached out and grabbed the man if he'd wanted to, wrapped his hands around that narrow throat and *squeezed*. But he didn't. Instead, Josef cleared his own throat and addressed him.

"Arbecht Heim." It wasn't a question.

The man started, then froze. Slowly, he turned to face Josef, and there was absolutely no doubt now. The swollen nose, the thin, white lips, one ear malformed, twisted, larger than the other. And those eyes. Old now, and tired, yes, but there was no mistaking those eyes. Arbecht Heim.

"*Schwein*," Josef said quietly, his voice vibrating with anger, and, he had to admit, not a little fear. "Pig." He was crying, but he would not realize this until later, when he reached up and felt the wetness on his cheeks. The man merely stared at him. He did not deny the accusation, but neither did he seem frightened, nor surprised. After a moment, he spoke.

"You know me then?"

"Indeed," Josef managed. "And you remember my names, yes? Kike. Christ-killer. Host-nailer. You knew them all." Arbecht Heim said nothing. "How is it I find you here, then?" Josef asked. "Strolling through this consumerist paradise without a care in the world, eh? Do you think the world has forgotten? I was so young then, so young. I do not remember Nuremberg. But when I was old enough to understand I read, I studied. You were not there. You had slipped through their fingers, escaping notice in the shadow of the Mengeles and the Himmlers.

"Yes," Heim whispered. "I escaped."

"And I, I am a stranger to you, aren't I?"

Heim shrugged wearily, and nodded.

"Then let me remind you," Josef said, stepping closer to the man, the monster. "I remember, when we got off the train, tired, scared. Me, my mama, my papa, my *schwester*. We were marched in a line past your men, and I saw *you* there, laughing and joking and flipping a coin. If the coin came up heads, you sent the person to work. If it came up tails, you sent them to the showers. The gas showers. That is what happened to my parents. Oh, but my sister, you did not flip your coin for her. You simply took her, and I did not see her again until that horrible day when you made us *dig*..."

Josef was trembling now, and for a moment he thought that he would simply attack Arbecht Heim, right here in the Woodsborough Shopping Plaza, and not relent until one or both of them were dead. Crazily, he wondered how the local news would handle the story of two decrepit old men fighting to the death at the local shopping mall on Christmas Eve. Doubtless, they would treat it as a joke. Two old fools fighting over the last copy of this year's hot new video game for their respective grandchildren. But Josef didn't care; he was fully prepared to assault this man, prepared to murder this man, prepared for almost anything but what Arbecht Heim did next.

"I do not remember," he said.

Josef was surprised to find himself speechless.

"What do you expect?" Heim continued. "There were so many, so very many. I cannot be expected to remember them all. But they recognize me. Some do not trust their eyes, do not believe that it could possibly be me after all this time, but enough have confronted me, spouted my horrors back at me, thrown my crimes in my face, spat on me, called me pig, dog. They curse me, sicken me with details of my horrific exploits, all committed in a time of madness in the name of a man long dead, and I cry *Enough!* but it never ends. I cringe every time I turn a corner, make eye contact with a stranger, because even after all this time there is always another... Eventually, there is always another."

"And yet you walk free, all these years later!" Josef was furious now, furious not only at Arbecht Heim, the monster, but at this parade of former victims who could have, should have, taken some sort of action. "You may have intimidated all the others, or garnered their pity, but I will *not* see you walk free! I will deliver you to the authorities myself, and you *will* burn in Hell for your crimes against humanity!" Arbecht Heim only looked sadder, smaller, more haunted.

"Touch me," he demanded.

And, not quite knowing why he obeyed, Josef reached gently out, only to feel his hand pass right through the Nazi, who was as insubstantial as a shadow.

"Don't you see?" Arbecht Heim said. "This *is* my Hell." He turned then, and within moments had disappeared into the bustling holiday crowd.

ABOUT THE AUTHOR

Brad D. Sibbersen has never tasted Spam.

ALSO BY THE AUTHOR

Welcome to Mad Science U
Bombed
The Princess That Ate Dragons
The Faerie Pit
Deadburbia
Night of the Hornéd God
Road Works: Four Tales
The World That Time Forgot
Involuntary
Everything Bad Happens to Jeremiah Riddle
Demons & Dragons
Amityville Subdivision
Graves Not Deep Enough
Look What's Happened to Mad Science U

9 798227 915177